TAKE MY PLACE

Other books by Beate Boeker:

Wings to Fly

TAKE MY PLACE

•

Beate Boeker

AVALON BOOKS

NEW YORK

Published by Thomas Bouregy & Co., Inc.
160 Madison Avenue, New York, NY 10016

Library of Congress Cataloging-in-Publication Data

Boeker, Beate.
    Take my place / Beate Boeker.
        p. cm.
    ISBN 978-0-8034-9942-3 (hardcover: acid-free paper)
1. Single mothers—Fiction.   2. Divorced women—Fiction.
I. Title.

PR9110.9.B64T35 2009
823'.914—dc22

                                        2008048218

PRINTED IN THE UNITED STATES OF AMERICA
ON ACID-FREE PAPER
BY HADDON CRAFTSMEN, BLOOMSBURG, PENNSYLVANIA

Chapter One

The black BMW convertible slid to a stop in front of her. Chris jumped out.

Maren watched him coming closer with her arms crossed in front of her chest. *He looks like a film star.* She narrowed her eyes. *Is it because of that ruffled hair and and his blue-green eyes?* Maren frowned. *No, it's the way he moves. He moves as if the world belongs to him.*

He took her hand and held it a moment longer than necessary. "I can't believe you waited."

"I didn't expect you any earlier." Maren made sure her voice sounded sweet.

His eyes widened. "But didn't we agree to meet at seven?"

She pretended to smile. "We did. But my experience told me you wouldn't make it."

"I tried to, Maren. I really did."

She eyed him, unconvinced.

"I lost my keys. It took me ages to hunt up my spare." He held up the key as if it was some kind of proof. "By the time I got to the dock, I'd missed the ferry by inches."

Maren couldn't suppress a grimace. How pat his excuses came.

He mistook it and smiled. "I've booked a table at Tony's. I'm looking forward to tonight."

Well, I'm not, Maren thought. *And even a table at Tony's won't reconcile me.*

With an inward sigh, Chris scanned the menu. Maren reminded him of an iceberg. Why did their fathers have to play golf at the same club? He couldn't afford to ruffle her feathers or he'd have to face some nasty consequences. His father had made that clear. If only she wasn't so straitlaced. As a rule, he never had trouble with women; on the contrary . . . but Maren always looked at him with a mixture of amusement and disdain that made him uncomfortable. Maybe his brother would be able to charm her. Surely the waiter had told Tony by now he was here.

The cell phone in his breast pocket began to vibrate. Darn. Maren wouldn't appreciate if he answered that call. She had shot him a look like a dagger when he'd answered a call during their business meeting last week. Heaven knew why. The hum got stronger.

It might be Kitty.

He had promised to answer.

Chris pushed back his seat with a fake smile at Maren. "I'll just wash my hands. I'll be back in a sec."

He retreated toward the back of the restaurant and ripped out his phone. "Hello?"

"Chris!" Kitty's voice sounded high and thin. "Thank God I reached you! You've got to come and help me—I lost it all, all, all! I don't know what to do anymore; I . . ."

"Hold on, Kitty! What happened?"

Kitty gulped. "My . . . my computer crashed, and it's all gone. All my work! I . . . I can't find the backup, and it's due on Monday, and I . . ." She started to cry.

Chris checked his watch. He couldn't leave Kitty in a hole, but he had that disgruntled iceberg waiting for him. Darn, darn, darn. He frowned and bit his lips. He had to find a way; he had to . . .

A thought shot through his head. Tony!

But no. Chris frowned. It was crazy.

Kitty's voice wobbled. "Chris, can you . . . can you come?"

Yes. It was crazy, but it was the only solution.

Chris took a deep breath. "Shhhh, Kitty, it's all right. I'll come and help you fix your computer, okay? But I'm on Bainbridge Island right now and have to wait for the next ferry."

"Bainbridge Island? But that's at the end of the world! I . . ." Kitty stopped mid sob. "Yes. I . . . thank you, Chris. I'll wait for you."

"See you soon." He hung up, turned on his heels, and stormed into the kitchen of the restaurant. For an instant, the white light blinded him. At the long wall in the back Tony's chef, Giovanni, and an assistant surveyed several pans sizzling over blue gas flames. The aroma of steak and onions made Chris' mouth water.

The assistant turned his head and Chris grinned at him. Must be a new guy; he had never seen him before. "Hi. I need my brother. Where's Tony?"

"Right here," Tony said behind him. "What's the panic?"

Chris swiveled around.

Tony stood in the small door that led to his office.

Thank God he was here. "Hi, Tony. I need your help."

The assistant stood frozen to the spot. He blinked, shook his head, and blinked again. Chris saw it from the corner of his eyes and couldn't suppress a chuckle. Always the same reaction—whenever people saw them together, they didn't trust their eyes.

Giovanni realized his assistant had turned into a statue and turned as well. When he discovered Chris standing next to Tony, a smile stretched across his broad face. "Hi, Chris." He nudged the assistant. "Can't see a difference, eh?" he said with a move of his chin toward the brothers.

Tony slapped Chris' back. "What's the matter, Chris? You look as if someone's haunting you."

Trust Tony to see through him. Chris pushed both hands through his hair and lowered his voice. "I'm here with a business partner, but Kitty just called. Her thesis is due on Monday, and her computer crashed. She's hysterical. I need to go and help her."

"So what's new?" Tony leaned against a gleaming steel table. "Kitty's been getting hysterical over some paper or other these last three years, hasn't she?"

Chris sighed. "Lord, don't I know it. But this is the last and most important one. I can't let her down."

"Right. And where do I come in?"

Chris lowered his voice even more so the sizzling would drown him out. "I thought we could switch roles, and you could take my place with my business contact, with Maren."

Tony stared at him, then pushed himself away from the table. "You're raving. I'm not going to do anything of the kind."

Chris hadn't expected a different answer. "Come on, Tony, be a sport."

Tony shook his head. He bent down, took a stainless steel bowl from a lower rack, and placed a bunch of carrots inside. "Why don't you explain the situation to that business partner of yours? I'm sure she'll understand."

"Not her," Chris said. "She'll wither me with a glance, and next thing I know, Dad will kick me out." That should convince Tony. He knew about the situation at the office.

Tony straightened and set the bowl with care on the table. "You know, I'm not sure that would be such a bad thing."

Chris wanted to stamp his foot. He had no time for a sermon. "It would be a disaster and you know it. Dad is still furious because you didn't follow the family tradition. I don't want to follow in your tracks and become the next victim of his wrath." He grinned. "I prefer him to be angry at you." Chris picked a carrot out of Tony's bowl and twirled it around his fingers. "Besides, I can't go to Maren and tell her she'll have to go home. It's the third time something's gone wrong and—"

"Hold on a minute," Tony held up his hand. "You're telling me this woman is angry at you?" He grabbed the carrot from Chris and put it back into the bowl.

Chris waved his hand. "Nothing you can't remedy with a bit of charm."

Tony shook his head. "You're mad."

Chris nudged Tony with his elbow. "Oh, come on. We've always stood in for each other, haven't we? Remember Greg's party?"

Tony shook his head. "That was years ago."

"But we can still do it." Chris nodded toward the assistant. "Even your assistant thought he was seeing double a minute ago. You know we can do it. It's just one night. She doesn't know me well."

Tony didn't reply. The assistant removed the sizzling pan from the fire, and all at once the kitchen was so quiet, it hummed through Chris' ears. Chris shifted his weight from one foot to the other. Why was Tony hesitating? They always stood in for each other.

The sounds of the restaurant came muffled through the green baize door. The clink of cutlery, the murmur of voices, and below everything, the melody of Mozart's Piano Concerto no. 19 in F Major.

He wished Tony would hurry. They'd fooled people so often. It was fun.

Something on the stove boiled over and hissed into the flames. Giovanni muttered an oath and rescued the pan from the fire.

Tony lifted his head with alarm as if he had just realized they weren't alone in the kitchen. He grabbed Chris' arm, drew him into his office, and closed the door with his foot. The music now came muted through the wall, but the smell of onions still hung in the air. A yellow lamp glowed above a rickety desk covered with bills and order forms. Chris blinked. How could Tony be happy in such a mouse hole?

Tony frowned. "You're sure . . . what's her name again?"

"Maren."

"What kind of a name is that?"

Chris sighed. "Her family is from Sweden. You pronounce it wrong, by the way. It's Mar-an."

Tony shook his head. "I'm sure this Mar-an will understand you have to go and help a friend."

"No chance."

"Hmm." Tony scratched his head. "Does it matter? If she complains, you just explain the situation to Dad.

You know how he harps on and on about his friends and how they always help each other. He'll understand you had to rescue Kitty."

Chris frowned. Why was Tony so slow on the uptake tonight? "He would, if Maren's father wasn't one of Dad's golf buddies. You know what happens if we make a golf buddy unhappy."

Tony sighed and rubbed his forehead. "Oh, no. You sure know how to pick 'em."

"Tony, come on, be a sport." Chris checked his watch. "Maren will think I left the island if we take much longer."

Tony took a deep breath. "All right. I'll do it under one condition."

Relief surged up in Chris. He grabbed Tony's hand. "Great! I knew you would do it. You know, you'll enjoy—"

Tony held up his hand. "I said under one condition."

Chris bent down and took off his shoes. "Come on, take off your stuff. I can't keep her waiting much longer. A condition? You want me to return a favor? Sure."

Tony didn't move. "I want you to quit your job at Dad's."

Chris laughed and straightened again. "Good joke." He eyed his brother's shirt. "You know what, mate, I'm not sure I care for that shirt of yours. But I guess I have to sacrifice myself."

"Chris. I wasn't joking. I believe you should quit. It's the wrong job for you. You hate it."

Chris threw his jacket across the shabby office chair and started to undo his shirt. "Hate my job? Hey, my convertible is part of it. How could I hate that?"

Tony didn't reply.

Chris kicked off his shoes. "Do I have to undress you myself? Move, man, or Maren will make a scene."

"Chris, I mean it. At least promise you'll think about it."

"Sure, I'll think about it. Now give me that hideous shirt, will you?"

Tony shook his head and sighed. "I have to go back to the kitchen first and invent some tale about why I have to leave. When you leave, just wave good-bye. Whatever you do, don't say anything or Guiseppe will know."

Chris grinned. "Don't worry. As if I would talk to Guiseppe. Who do you take me for? A beginner?"

Tony slammed the door shut behind him but came back a minute later. "So what do I need to know about this Mar-an?"

Chris waved a hand. "She's a consultant and helps people set up new businesses. Make sure you don't talk shop. She'll know after three words you're faking it."

Tony unbuttoned his shirt and threw it toward his brother. "Anything special I should talk about?"

"I don't know." Chris picked up the shirt with his fingertips and frowned at it. "You know what? I'll give you a decent shirt for your birthday." He shrugged it on. "She's not a talker, rather cool sometimes."

"Perfect." Tony bent down to undo his shoelaces.

"Of course you go out with the one woman in the world who doesn't like talking." He frowned at his socks. "Do we have to exchange those too?"

"You bet. Women notice the strangest things." Chris held out his hands.

Tony handed over his socks. "What else? Is she married? Children? Hobbies?"

Chris stopped in the middle of putting on a sock and frowned. "You know, I have no clue."

"Does that mean she never told you or you can't remember?"

Chris shrugged. "I'm not sure . . . I think she never told me. Really, Tony, you worry too much. You'll see; it's easy. And tomorrow, we'll have a laugh about it together." He slapped his brother's back and laughed. "After all, she has no idea I've got a twin."

"Let's hope so." Tony pulled on Chris' shirt. "Does she have a little habit of running amok from time to time?"

"Not at all." Chris closed Tony's trousers. "You've lost weight, Tony."

"No, you got fat. So she's amiable and easygoing?"

"I wouldn't say so." Chris shrugged. "But you can count on one thing: She never loses control. Even in a white-hot fury, she will calmly look for the right weapon before she attacks."

Tony tied his shoelaces and straightened. "What a comforting thought."

"It won't be long. After dinner, you can drop her at the ferry. She's got her car there."

"Fine. I need your car keys. You'll find mine in the drawer at the desk."

Chris pulled his keys out of his pocket and threw them to his brother. "This is fun, isn't it? I wish I could watch you both tonight."

Tony pushed him toward the desk. "Oh, hush up and go help Kitty."

Chris laughed, fished his brother's keys from the drawer, and went to the door. Just as he touched the door handle, he stopped and turned. "I forgot one thing. Whatever you do, don't forget to look at her ankles. They're worth it."

Tony rolled his eyes. "Great. That's all I need to make the evening a success."

When Tony opened the door, he almost ran into his waiter Shaun. Chris held his breath. Tony squared his shoulders and winked at him. "You won't mention I was in my brother's kitchen, will you?"

"No, sir."

Chris grinned behind Tony's back. It still worked.

Maren frowned and checked her watch. What on earth had happened to Chris? She glanced toward the rear of the restaurant. Nothing. Maybe some stomach trouble? A sudden illness?

With a sigh, she shook her head. Not likely. How many times had she waited in vain for him? Three times? Four? Maren bit her lips. But leaving her high and dry in the middle of a fine restaurant was a first, even for him. She shouldn't have agreed to this dinner. How many tax consultants lived in Seattle? A thousand? Nine hundred ninety-nine had a better attitude than Chris. Oh, well, maybe nine hundred, but still . . .

Maren looked out the window across the glittering water of the sound. The soft June evening light smoothed every harsh angle until the whole world looked like a lilac dream. Across Elliott Bay she could discern the first lights on the Seattle skyline, springing up here and there, as if an invisible wizard touched the buildings with his magic stick.

But where was that man? Maren sighed again and frowned.

What had Annie said, just half an hour ago, when she had met her at the ferry, sitting on the pier and waiting for Chris?

"Why do you have to work with an unreliable tax consultant?"

"He's from Mountforth and Adams." Maren watched Annie out of the corner of her eye to see if she would react like everybody else.

She did by whistling, a startling sound to come from her wrinkled lips. "Ah. A big name."

Maren nodded. "And a big reputation. Since I'm new to the business, it helps to say I work with them . . . gives me some sort of respectability."

"I see." Annie turned her head. "But that's not all."

Maren grinned and swung her foot. "Aren't my new shoes great?"

"They're foolish. How on earth do you manage to walk on such high heels?"

"I don't walk, I trip. Trip, trip, trip. Like a little fairy lady. At least, that's what Sherry says."

Annie made a short grating sound in her throat and Maren gave her a quick hug. "Yes, yes, I know I shouldn't change the subject, and yes, you are right. There is something else to it. He's good-looking and charming."

"Oh, dear. Good-looking, charming, and unreliable."

Maren put her head to one side and smiled. "Yes, that about sums him up."

"Don't tell me you've fallen for a guy like that? You always used to be so sensible."

"No. I haven't fallen for him. I use him. I impress my customers by walking in with a guy who looks like Mr. Gorgeous. Next I tell them he's from Mountforth and Adams. And then I drop the information that he's the son of the owner."

Annie shook her head. "And then you drop that he forgets dates."

"Well." Maren concentrated on her foot again. "That's the hitch. I think I will have to drop him altogether. Soon. I can't afford mistakes. He stood me up on a date with a new client earlier in the week. And the week before, he messed up a file."

"And yet you say he's not stupid."

Maren sighed. "I think he's unhappy. That's why I agreed on a business dinner. Maybe I can find out what's bothering him. I don't want to stop working with Mountforth and Adams. The name opens doors, believe me."

Annie made another sound in her throat. "You're too softhearted. If he's not doing his job, find someone else. There are other tax accountants in Seattle. Are you sure he hasn't bewitched you a little?"

A white motorboat putt-putted by and rippled the smooth surface of the water. Maren crossed her ankles, leaned back, and held her face toward the waning sun. "Positive. The man is like an eel. Every time you try to start a serious conversation, he makes a joke and switches the topic. I wish I could nail him down just once. I have yet to hear a single honest reply from him."

Annie nodded at the hazy skyline of Seattle across the Bay. "At least you chose a beautiful waiting point."

"Yes. I figured the chances were fifty-fifty he'd miss the ferry. Though I admit I expected him to make an effort. After all, I made it clear I've had more than enough of his sloppy attitude." She pointed across the sound. "But look, the next ferry will dock in ten minutes. If he's not on it, I'll contact another tax consultant on Monday."

Annie shook her head so hard, her earrings started to tingle. "I advise you to do so right now. A leopard doesn't change its spots."

Maren shook her head to clear it and checked the rear of the restaurant once again. Still no sign of Chris. Unbelievable. On the table in front of her, fresh rose petals floated in a dark red bowl. She touched one petal with her finger tip. It felt like velvet. Of course Annie had been right. Annie had always been right, even back then, when she had advised her not to marry Brad.

Maren checked her watch. Twenty past eight. Brad would have put Sherry into her bed at the Sorrento Hotel already. At least she hoped so. Had they spent a nice day at the Seattle zoo? Had Sherry felt familiar with her dad? Would she be so impressed by his glittering world that her home would now seem boring? Something clenched inside Maren. She swallowed, bent forward, and smelled the rose. It reminded her of her wedding bouquet. Sweet and promising. Maren sighed. Seven years. It was seven years ago. How glad she was to be independent now. It had given her quite a jolt when Brad had called yesterday. How many times had he come to see their daughter? Five, six? Of course, he lived in Texas, but still . . . Maren shook her head. Sherry would come home tomorrow. It was funny, she longed so often to have a bit of time just for herself, but now that Sherry was away, she felt lonely. Even the lump of bright red modeling clay Sherry had thrown so hard against the ceiling that morning that it still stuck gave her an aching feeling inside.

Maren shook herself. Her work left little time for being lonely. She grinned when she thought of Annie's reply to her latest project. "You know what I did last week?" Maren said.

"Well?" Annie's earrings blinked in the sun.

"I sent a query to Henry Barker Productions."

Annie stared at her. "Henry who?"

Maren laughed. "Oh, Annie, you know him. He's doing the show on TV called *Noteworthy Enterprises.* If they took me on, my company profile and story would be broadcast all over the West Coast." The thought alone made her stomach flutter.

"That sounds good."

"Yeah. But probably he won't even bother to reply."

Annie looked at her and hesitated. She seemed to want to say something, then stopped herself. Out on the water, a seagull hung in the sky and waggled on the spot like a puppet on strings. A waft of tang and sea water played on the pier. Annie stretched out her hand and touched Maren's arm. "Don't look like that, dear. I think it's courageous, the way you tackle your new job."

Maren swallowed. "I'm still with my back to the wall, Annie. I know Mom and Dad will always support me if I need it, but I don't want to take any more money from them."

"You will make it. Don't worry. I know it for sure."

Maren felt a small glow of warmth. "Thank you, Annie. It's nice to know someone believes in me."

Annie hoisted herself up. "I have to go. Good luck in reforming the leopard, my dear. If you have the time, drop in for a cup of coffee. Bring Sherry too."

Maren jumped up and gave her another hug. "You know you're welcome anytime at my house too. You've never seen it."

Annie shook her head. "I'm sorry. The last few months at the hospital were crazy."

"Well, drop in when you have a minute." Maren grinned. "I promise to tell you all about my progress with the leopard."

A waiter rushed by with a sizzling steak. It smelled delicious. Maren scanned the restaurant. If Chris didn't show up within one minute, she would have no progress at all to report to Annie because she would have left before his return. Hot anger started to pulsate through her just as a man emerged from the back of the restaurant and stepped into the warm light.

Chris.

Finally!

He seemed a bit pale. Maren frowned. Maybe she shouldn't mention the long wait after all.

Chapter Two

Tony came to his brother's table and slid into the seat. *Do I look as uptight as I feel?* He tried a smile. "Sorry to be so long."

The woman in front of him glanced up and smiled. "No problem."

Tony suffered a shock. After Chris' description, he had expected someone tough, someone with one eye on the watch, someone harsh and angular. In disbelief, he stared at her curved mouth and the thick chestnut hair loosely clasped together at the back of her neck. A tendril had escaped, and the candlelight on the table threw its soft shadow on her cheek.

With an effort, he murmured something and opened the menu he knew by heart. Panic gripped him. How was he going to pull it off?

She made a move of her hands toward the menu. "The menu is mouthwatering. I can't make up my mind."

He had to concentrate. He had to make sense.

She still looked at the menu. "Is there anything you can recommend?"

Thank God, a question he had answered a thousand times before. It put him back on track. He started to list his favorites with a voice that didn't seem to belong to him.

She listened with her head bent to one side, then said, "I believe I'll take the tuna steak. It sounds wonderful. I'm addicted to spinach."

Tony smiled. "Sounds like a good choice."

When Shaun came to their table, they placed their orders. Tony surveyed him from beneath lowered lids and was glad Shaun didn't show by so much as a twisting muscle they had met before. He also moved with dexterity and ease. Yes, it had been the right decision to employ him. Maybe he should test all his waiters like that.

As Tony chose the wine, he felt as if he had stepped into a movie. It was such a strange feeling to be a guest in his own restaurant. Maybe he should do it more often. It showed things from a different perspective. His chair creaked when he moved. He would have to see to that.

What on earth was he going to say to the poised woman in front of him? She wanted red wine in spite of having chosen fish. What did that make her? A culinary Philistine? An independent mind? He looked at her and wondered what Chris would say, but his mind was a blank. He swallowed. When had he last gone out with a beautiful woman? He couldn't remember.

She smiled at him. Really, she had the happiest mouth he'd ever seen, wide and curved. After Chris' description, he had expected someone with prim, tight lips. How did she look when she laughed?

Maren leaned back in her chair and lifted her glass. "Cheers." She swirled the fiery red liquid in her glass in small circles, inhaled, and took a slow sip. Her face lit up. "The wine is good."

He smiled. So she knew something about wine. "I'm glad you like it. The year 2002 was especially good for the Insignia Napa Valley wine." Gosh, he sounded like a textbook.

Maren nodded. "I've never tasted this year before but I visited their winery in 2000."

"You did? So did I. The year before, though."

"I loved it." Maren took another small sip. "Once you know about the winemaking process and how much work goes into it, you drink wine with a different mind, don't you? It's almost . . . almost a piece of art."

"Absolutely." Tony relaxed. Maybe Chris had been right, and it would be easy. If she knew how to savor food, he could spend the whole evening without running out of things to say.

He stole another look at her. How could Chris have been impervious to her charm?

She looked up. He smiled at her, and she smiled back.

Confidence eased his tense shoulders. Easy. It was easy.

Maren put her chin in her hand, turned the stem of her glass with the other, and looked at the dark red liquid. What was she thinking about?

Suddenly, she lifted her head and met his eyes. "You're different tonight."

Oh, no. He caught his breath. "Really?" His voice sounded strange. "How?"

"I don't know." She contemplated her glass. "Somehow . . . calmer. More centered."

If she sensed a difference after such a short time, how was he going to make it through dinner? Had he just thought it was easy? Famous last words. He forced himself to smile. "Choosing the right dinner takes a lot of concentration."

Her eyes twinkled. "I guess it does. Particularly if the choice makes dreaming unnecessary."

He swallowed. She couldn't have paid him a bigger compliment.

"You know," Maren said, "you can always tell when a business is done with love . . . it shows in a hundred different ways."

He looked at his restaurant and tried to see it through her eyes. The view through the panorama windows was spectacular; every guide mentioned that. From the edge of the island, they looked out toward the skyline of Seattle. He had fallen in love with the view long before he had dared to dream about opening a restaurant.

He remembered the agony he'd felt when it came to the inside of the restaurant. He hated the stark modern places where every word fell onto a hard floor and reverberated off the concrete walls, but neither did he go for the old pub style with loads of oak where the customers had to grope in the dark to find their drink. After hours spent over magazines, he gave up in despair and asked an interior decorator friend for help. And in a few minutes, or so it had seemed to him, she developed a concept he loved from the start. She found a brocade material for the upholstery and curtains in a rich burgundy tone that filled the room with warmth and elegance. Combined with simple cherrywood tables polished to a dark sheen, the room breathed harmony. For everything else, she chose silver and glistening linen. "If you stick to silver and white from now on, you can't go wrong," she had given him as a guideline when they had finished.

"Just look at the way the napkin is folded." Maren's voice interrupted his thoughts. "Nestled inside is this little card, have you seen it?" With her fingertips, she extracted an engraved card made of stiff, creamy cardboard. It had two slim lines at the short side, one silver, one burgundy, and the name *Tony's* in the middle. "I remember I took it with me when my mother and father invited me here six months ago, to celebrate the beginning of my company."

Oh, no. She had been in his restaurant before? Had she seen him?

He frowned. Six months ago . . . it might have been during his short vacation last winter. Yes. He dared to take another breath.

Maren still looked at the card. "I stuck it on my mirror and each time I look at it, it evokes a little of the exhilarated feeling I had that evening—a mix of pride and happiness and the memory of scrumptious food." She smiled. "And whenever I see the logo *Tony's,* I connect it with something wonderful. That's clever marketing, don't you think?"

He could not trust his voice to speak, so he nodded.

She looked up and smiled with that irresistible mouth of hers. "Is there really a Tony who owns this place?"

He had to tell her. If she found out afterward, it would seem strange if he hadn't mentioned it.

"Yes." He cleared his throat. "And he would be touched by your praise."

"Oh, well, I guess he hears stuff like that all the time."

"No." Tony took a deep breath. "He doesn't."

She lifted her eyebrows. "You know him?"

Tony nodded and looked into his glass. He moved it a little and watched the soft waves of the red wine cling to the smooth glass, then slither down toward the center. "He's my brother."

"Your brother!" Her eyes widened. "Didn't you once tell me you're a respected family of lawyers and tax experts ever since Chief Seattle?"

Tony smiled. "We are. You can't imagine the uproar when"—he hesitated—"Tony announced he was going to be a cook. Father thought it was a disgrace and Mother imagined him doing hamburgers in a greasy kitchen till kingdom come."

"But that's what it is," she said.

"No, it's not!" He was surprised by the stab of pain he felt. Surely he should have overcome that old feeling of standing with his back to the wall every time he mentioned his profession. He hadn't expected it from her, though. Not after what she'd said earlier.

At that moment, Shaun appeared at their table with the appetizers they had ordered. "Here's the grilled zucchini with goat cheese." He placed a fluted silvery dish in front of them. "The sun-dried tomatoes should be taken with the fresh bread and the black olives right here." He conjured up another twinkling dish. "And this is the salmon carpaccio with the tangerine vinaigrette." He smiled at them. "Enjoy your meal."

"So it's hamburgers in a greasy kitchen?" Tony indicated the table with his hand.

"Not now," she said. "But it is in the beginning. Don't tell me it's not. I bet your brother hated it when he started out."

He remembered his first weeks. Cutting onions had

been his one and only occupation, scarcely relieved by a welcome batch of lemons, and whenever he remembered the chef who had terrorized them all, he still shuddered. "It was horrible," he admitted. "I—um—he would have thrown in the towel, but he had to prove himself."

"Don't we all?" she said.

It was on the tip of his tongue to ask her where she had to prove herself, but just in time, he remembered to hold back. Darn Chris. He could not ask a single thing without running the risk of blowing his cover.

But it was nice to watch her eat. She placed a piece of goat cheese on her fork, balanced it to her mouth, and just as she started to chew, she closed her eyes for a second. If she did everything as thoroughly as she ate, the clash between her and his happy-go-lucky brother was inevitable. He had to smile at the thought.

She looked up and met his eyes.

Stillness enveloped them. The sounds of the restaurant receded, and a firework started in his stomach.

A hint of color crept into her cheeks. She looked at her plate again.

He breathed faster. She really had the most inviting mouth. For one crazy instant he wondered how it would feel to kiss her. He had to stop that thought. Now! He had to talk to her. "Um . . . ah . . . have you ever been to the Seattle Zoo?"

Great, Tony. Wonderful topic. Did he want to discuss elephants and gorillas for the rest of the evening?

She gave him a funny look. "Not recently, no. But I remember I loved it."

"So did I." Tony fell silent. Darn. If she hadn't given him that funny look, he might have talked about their favorite animals, but she probably already thought he was odd.

They continued to eat in silence.

Maren bit into the last piece of bread with obvious pleasure. "How did your brother come to open a restaurant?"

"It was for sale at an auction." He was glad to talk about something neutral. "Everything was in ruins, but the view made it just right."

"How did he put up the money?"

He blinked. What an odd question. "I—um—he went to our father and borrowed it."

"Courageous."

"To borrow money from your parents?" He laughed without mirth. "Most would call that the easy way out."

"Depends on the parents," Maren said. "Sometimes it's easier to go to a bank and get a loan with interest rates from someone who won't comment on your every step."

Tony smiled. She seemed to know something about it. "Tony was scared stiff," he said. "He worked like crazy those first years. Partly to fulfill his dream, partly haunted by his debts."

"And in spite of it all I bet he's happier than you are."

He recoiled. If she kept dropping bombs like that, he

was going to have a heart attack before the night was out. "What on earth do you mean?"

There was Shaun again, like a genie out of a bottle. Did he have to interrupt them all the time?

"The tuna steak with creamed spinach and basmati rice . . ." He placed the plate in front of Maren. ". . . and the lamb chop with brussels sprouts and roasted potatoes."

When he had left, Tony frowned at Maren without picking up his fork. "Why do you think I'm unhappy?"

"Aren't you?"

"I asked you first." He was not going to give her an inch.

"It's hard to put a finger on it." She leaned her head to one side and chose her words with care. "I have the impression you are"—she hesitated—"restless and . . . and not happy with what you do. Though it doesn't show as much as usual tonight."

He stared at her. He had watched his brother for some time already, noting the signs of restlessness with misgiving. He suffered with Chris and knew he had to change something. But it was one thing if he saw through his twin brother, and quite another if a woman who was barely acquainted with him did so too. Was it that obvious? If so, it was high time Chris did something about it. It made him feel better about having asked Chris to reconsider his job tonight, but at the same time, he felt uncomfortable with that clairvoyant woman in front of him.

"Are you the elder?" she asked.

Tony started to shake his head, then nodded. *By as much as fifteen minutes*, he thought.

"Do you have any other brothers or sisters?"

"No."

"Well," she said, pushing a piece of tuna, some spinach, and rice onto her fork, "maybe you felt the strain of doing the expected thing more than your younger brother, and that's why you became a tax consultant like your father."

He stared at her, and as the words sank in, he understood the implication. "Listen," he felt angry for Chris, "are you trying to tell me I'm no good as a tax consultant?"

Her fork clattered onto the table and her eyes widened, but she did not look away. "I'm sorry. I didn't want to hurt you."

"That's no answer."

"Well, no." She stared at him.

"Why do you look so confused? Did you expect another reaction?" He wanted to get to the bottom of it. She did not make sense. On the one hand, her face, with its frank gaze, couldn't be completely misleading; he liked the way she enjoyed her food and how she had talked about his restaurant. On the other hand, she had made those harsh remarks about being a cook and now about Chris' job. It did not go together, she couldn't be so sensitive one minute and so unsubtle the next. It was as if she meant to provoke him, as if . . . he stopped in the middle of his thought.

"That's it, isn't it?" he said. He bent forward and fixed her. "You're trying to provoke me." He remembered his brother's words. "You're trying to find out where it hurts most."

Chapter Three

She looked as if he had slapped her face. "I'm not."

"You could have fooled me." His gaze never left her face. "How about telling me the truth?"

Maren stared at him without saying a word.

"Come on, tell me."

Maren bit her lip and took a deep breath. "I'm not sure if I can verbalize it. It might hurt you—and me—and . . . I'd hate to make you bitter."

He had no clue what she meant. "Try me."

She took a sip of her wine and folded her hands into a tight ball in front of her. "All right."

Another pause.

She seemed to wrestle with something. Finally, she said: "Do you know your most prominent characteristic?"

"Well?"

"You're untouchable."

He lifted his eyebrows.

"Yes, you are. No matter what is said to you, you will always find a charming answer. No matter what has gone wrong, you will find a loophole to get out."

He heard the bitterness in her voice. "Is that bad?"

"No." She shook her head. Suddenly, she looked tired. "Not at all. But suppose someone depends on you, and . . . and you fail to do what you promised to do." She lifted her gaze. "You leave me with an annoyed customer and walk out, a joke on your lips." She made an impatient movement with her hands. "Sorry, that sounds way too melodramatic."

His mouth was dry. He knew exactly what she was talking about. She had sketched Chris, ever charming Chris, all right.

Maren took another deep breath. "And because I was—am—bitter about the times you left me high and dry, I looked for something that might touch you. I wanted to get behind your wall of sunshine; I wanted to see if anybody lives there."

He opened his mouth but before he could say something, she reached out and touched his hand. "But I never looked for weak points to hurt you. In fact, I've only now realized why I tried to provoke you."

She folded her hands again and stared at her white knuckles. "You're different tonight. You're not behind that wall at all. I didn't realize it in time. And when you challenged my words, you scared me to death." She lifted her gaze to his. Her lips curved upward. "I wasn't prepared for such a dramatic change. It's as if you are a different person tonight."

He almost told her then. Darn Chris and his schemes. She did not deserve to be deceived. She made herself so vulnerable, and he played a part. But before he could open his mouth, she continued. "I don't think you're happy in your job, Chris. You're bored out of your skull. Why do you stick with it even though your brother has realized his dream?"

"Maren," he said. It was the first time he said her name, and it propelled him into a world where only the two of them existed. But when their eyes met, he couldn't squeeze out a word.

If he told her he was sorry for the way Chris behaved, in what kind of light would it appear tomorrow, once she knew she had not been talking to Chris at all?

No. He could say nothing, do nothing. Not yet. Not tonight. He would have to force Chris to come clean tomorrow . . . and hope she'd forgive them. "I need to tell you something. But I can only do so tomorrow." Should he admit someone else was involved? No, that was too close to the truth; she was too clever for that. "Will you wait?"

She frowned and scanned his face. After a while, a smile crept into her eyes and she said, "I will."

He wanted to touch that tendril of hair, smooth it away from her cheek. Tony clenched his teeth and forced himself to look away. If he wanted to keep sane, he had to steer the talk toward safe topics—places they had seen, memories, favorite foods. It wasn't hard to make her talk, and it wasn't hard to listen. But whenever he thought about their evening, he only remembered her face. He remembered how the candlelight threw shadows on her cheeks; he remembered the mobility of her mouth, and how it twisted something inside him; he remembered the tendril swinging with her every move.

When he put her scarf around her shoulders as they were leaving, her scent floated up to him, a hint of orange and jasmine. He forced his hands away from her and followed her into the night like a man in a dream.

Maren glanced at Chris as she walked toward his car. A sudden gust of wind whipped the firs behind the building and filled the night with a fresh smell of pine, but she felt warm and light. A deep happiness hummed inside her. Her words to Annie just a few hours earlier made her chuckle; she had claimed to be impervious to his charm. Talk about famous last words. How could a few hours make such a difference? How come she had never noticed the smile in his eyes? How come she had never been able to talk to him like that before, easy, relaxed, just being herself? Next to the warm glow of happiness, she felt a tinge of fear. She had no time for romance. She was so glad she had finally settled in her single life, settled herself, Sherry, her job. She had no time for upheaval, no time for change. Most of all, she had no time to get hurt.

Maren shook her head and gave herself a little shake. *Enjoy the evening*, she told herself. *And don't worry about tomorrow. Carpe diem. You know what that means, right?*

In the car, she turned a little in her seat to watch his face. A street lamp threw its light on him, then darkness hid him again. The car smelled of leather and after-shave. A large advertising sign—was it Coca-Cola?—filled the interior with garish red light.

In one blinding moment of truth, she knew she trusted him blindly. Amazing. When a few hours ago, she would not have trusted him to post a letter. She smiled to herself when it happened.

The car came to stop at a red light. A bright street light lit up the interior. She saw his profile cut out against the light, the way his hands touched the steering wheel, the angle he held his head. And all of a sudden, he did not look like Chris at all, but like a stranger she had never met before.

Maren caught her breath. She did not hear the sound of the motor anymore, nor smell the leather seat beneath her. The colors faded out of her world and left it black and white. She blinked and willed the picture to shift right back, pushed away the feeling of strangeness. But it did not change. He looked different. Not like Chris . . . no, not like Chris at all.

The street light changed to green, and he accelerated with confidence, but not in his usual style. On the way to the restaurant, Chris had raced his car as if being chased, even if the next red light was only a few yards away. Now, he didn't. As if he was someone else.

She swallowed. *Maybe I'm losing my mind. Maybe I won't recognize Sherry next. Or myself. Maybe I'm splitting apart.* She stared at the back of her hand, the shape of her fingers. Everything looked familiar, like always. A wave of relief washed over her.

Maren twisted in her seat and stared at him. It was a trick of the light. It had to be.

But at the next stop, he turned and smiled at her, and no doubt remained. The man next to her wasn't Chris. Maren shrank back into the darkness of her corner.

She couldn't tell how she knew. She couldn't point a finger at it; it was just a sum of little things, each too small to list.

Suddenly, she remembered a voice she couldn't put a face to. Had it been Paula, the receptionist at his office? They had joked one day about Chris and good-looking men, and Paula had said: "And then to imagine they exist in doubles." Maren had laughed but had not been able to ask anything because Chris had arrived that instant.

So the man next to her was his twin. Tony. The brother who owned the restaurant . . . if she could believe the story he had told her tonight.

She went through every scene at the restaurant again. It was so obvious, once she knew. When had the change taken place? She recalled the evening step-by-step. Of course—it must have been right at the beginning, before they had even ordered. That's why he had been gone such a long time.

If she thought about the things she'd said to him! . . . Maren winced. How he must have laughed at her. And the look in his eyes, which seemed so intense, as if nobody else existed—it must have been because he was checking if she would see through the masquerade.

Her throat hurt. Tomorrow, he would tell Chris everything, and they would laugh at their clever game. She found herself shaking.

She threw another look at him. Everything had changed within the last thirty seconds, but he had no clue. She tried to take a deep breath but her chest was too tight. Maren curled up as much as she could. Her stomach felt cold and hard.

From far off, she heard Tony say, "Are you cold? I'll turn on the heat."

She did not reply. How dare he? How dare they do this to her? Those good-looking, ever-winning twins. Fooling the world so they got what they wanted. Always. And to imagine she had fallen like a ton of bricks for his brother, when Chris was no danger to her. It was so humiliating. And it hurt. Oh, but why? Why do it at all?

The radiator heated up the car. Maren still felt cold. Every muscle inside her bunched up, every bone ached.

Fury rose within her. The twins were not going to get away with it.

"Maren?" His voice sounded dark and soft. "You're awfully quiet all of a sudden."

She cleared her throat. Now she knew how to take her revenge . . . she would make him sweat tonight. "I was thinking what a shame it would be to go home so early." She forced her voice to sound light and fluffy.

"I see."

Ha! No enthusiasm there. No wonder. He probably thought he had finished his job with top marks. He would have a second thought coming.

"Yes!" She tried to sound like Paula the receptionist, who always reminded her of a canary on drugs. "Don't you think that would be fun?" She had to be careful not to overdo it.

Tony cleared his throat. "Would you like to go dancing?"

No. Certainly not. It would mean getting much too close. Besides, there was no opportunity for talk. And talk he would. She would squeeze him out like a lemon. She would make him squirm, make him as uncomfortable as she felt.

"Weeeell." She drew out the word. "I don't know. Don't you know something a little quieter?" She felt herself blush in the dark. Great. Now he would think she wanted to go to bed with him. Hastily, she added: "A drink somewhere?"

He nodded, turned right, and accelerated. "I know

just the right place." She could hear the satisfaction in his voice. "I'm sure you'll like it."

Maren shuddered. *Like heck I will.*

The moon glimmered on the smooth surface of the water. A ripple appeared and broke the light until the black surface looked as if someone had tossed a thousand sparkling gems onto it. The sky arched in a velvety blue, just one shade lighter than the murmuring sea. Far across the bay, lights dotted the skyline of Seattle.

Maren laid back her head until it touched the cabin wall and watched the star-spangled sky. The longer she looked, the more stars she discovered. They seemed to be coming closer now. She folded her hands around her knees and breathed the salty air, so mild tonight. If only the weight on her chest would go away.

She heard Tony coming along the deck, but she didn't move. Without a word, he glided beside her onto the thick waterproof cushions that ran all along the cabin wall. He did not touch her. Given the darkness and the limited space, it would have been more natural if he had brushed against her. Maren felt angry with herself for regretting it. Why should she feel attracted to him, after all she knew? She had always been able to rely on her brain. But for some reason, tonight was different, as if brain and body followed different rules. Why did Tony's presence create a turmoil inside her while his twin brother didn't tweak a single nerve?

Maren took a deep breath. It seemed a shame to destroy a mellow summer night, but even if he took her out on a romantic midnight trip along the coast, she would not lose sight of her revenge. But oh, wouldn't it be nice to just let go and lean her head against his shoulder? It was so near. If only he had not deceived her. If only they had met under different circumstances. How could a few hours make such a difference to her peace of mind?

Tony looked at her. "What are you thinking of?"

Maren swallowed. She kept her gaze on the stars. *Make him sweat*, she thought. "I've been thinking about Jill Spencer's contract. I believe there is a hitch that might present a problem if she ever decides to—"

"Maren," he said, "don't talk about work. You can talk all week about work, but not tonight. This boat wasn't made for work. It's a leisure boat, and it will be unhappy if we try to turn it into a business boat."

She had to smother a smile in spite of her exasperation. Darn him and his twin. "Just one small problem to get off my chest." She turned her head. "Don't you think it might leave her more room for future development if you change the status of the company to—"

"Listen . . . ," he said.

With satisfaction, she heard the harassed tone in his voice.

". . . it's not healthy to work at midnight."

"Really?" Maren made sure her voice sounded like silk. "I guess your brother suffers a lot then, at the restaurant?"

"He's used to it." He pointed toward the horizon. "Why don't you just enjoy the stars?"

She would love to. But if she gave in now, he would laugh at her tomorrow, together with his hateful brother. "Why are you always late?" she asked.

Silence. She knew he was fighting for words. He could not promise Chris would improve, and he wasn't as apt as his brother in inventing smooth lies.

Let him suffer. Why had he agreed to cover his twin?

Finally, he said, "Things will change. I promise."

How different they were. Chris would never have given a serious reply, let alone a promise. He would have countered each hit with a laugh and a fun remark, choosing to ignore her attack. Yes, they were different, these brothers. But they were brothers anyway, and they had bonded together to make her a fool.

Maren pushed down her feeling of guilt and said, "Well, time will show the value of that promise. By the way, I'm still waiting for your answer concerning the Smith documents." She held her breath. The Smith documents didn't exist. She was almost one hundred percent sure the man next to her wasn't Chris, but this was the ultimate test. If he refused any knowledge of the Smith documents . . .

He took a deep breath. "Maren, please, let it go. Can't we talk on Monday about them? Look at the sky. Feel the breeze. How can you go on about the Smith documents at such a moment?"

Maren narrowed her eyes, and her exasperation with

Chris foamed over. "I can go on about my work at any given moment, because I happen to be enthusiastic about it. I also happen to be the owner of a one-woman company, and therefore, I'm under more pressure than a son in his father's well-established company."

Tony flinched.

Maren felt like a louse. *But he deserves to be punished!* Hopefully, he was going to take it out on his brother tomorrow . . . who would deny all knowledge of the famous Smith documents.

"Maren." His voice sounded determined, as if he had made a decision.

Would he confess? Her heart lifted. If he did, she would forgive him quicker than lightning. She might even enjoy the stars. They might stay on his enchanted boat until sunrise, until . . . She caught herself. "Yes?"

"Tell me about myself."

"What?"

"Tell me how you see me. You mentioned at the restaurant I'm no good at my job. Why not?"

She averted her face. The twins were worlds apart. The last thing Chris would ever want was the truth. Didn't Tony know that? She shook her head. "I've already told you."

"Tell me again."

Strange. But if he wanted to hear the truth, he would get it. Without any decorative side dishes.

She sat up straight. "All right. But don't blame me if you hear things you don't want to hear." She took a deep breath. "You forget deadlines. You never call back. You tell lies when you're in a tight spot." She looked out over the velvet blue sea. "You're sure you want me to go on?"

"Yes." It sounded as if he spoke through clenched teeth.

"You think because you're good-looking and charming, rules don't apply to you." She paused, then added, "You're not interested in tax issues."

He didn't reply but stared out at the sea with hunched shoulders.

She wondered what he was thinking. "You want more?"

He turned his head. "Why on earth do you continue to work with . . . me?"

"Mountforth and Adams is a well-known company. Its reputation is good for me. But to be honest, I'm thinking of switching soon."

"Don't." His voice sounded hoarse.

She shrugged. "Somebody recently told me a leopard doesn't change its spots. I'd rather have a brilliant business partner with no reputation at all than one who relies entirely on his father's achievements."

She shot a look at him. The expression on his face hit a raw place in her soul. And although everything she said was the truth, she would never have hit it over his head if his masquerade hadn't hurt so much. But enough was enough. Revenge was a dangerous game. Annie once said it came back to destroy the destroyer. She hugged herself. "Take me back to my car, please."

Without a word, he got up and started the motor.

She had never felt so miserable.

It happened when he helped her ashore. Somehow, the heel of her shoe, her attractive new shoe, got caught on the edge of the pier and stuck. Her right ankle turned at an impossible angle. With a cry, she fell down. "Ouch!"

"What's the matter?"

"Nothing." She tried to get up but pain shot like hot liquid up her ankle. With a gasp, she fell back again.

A lantern on the boat next to them illuminated the spot where she had fallen. Tony knelt down and took her foot in his hands.

The warmth of his fingers sent a tremble up her spine, and to her surprise, tears spilled out of her eyes. "It's nothing." Her voice shook.

"Good thing your shoe is not more than two straps. We won't have any trouble taking it off." With infinite care, he opened the slim strap and eased off her shoe. Maren bit her lips to keep them from trembling. She didn't want him to see her losing control.

"There." Their eyes met. His face softened, and he bent forward and touched her cheek. "That was the worst of it. I'll take you to Poulsbo. They've got a medical center." He frowned. "I'm not sure if there's a closer one. Maybe . . ."

His touch turned her heart upside down. Where was her brain? "You don't have to take me anywhere." She hoped he didn't hear the catch in her voice. "I'll be fine. Let's just wait a minute."

They waited in silence. Her ankle swelled as she watched it, but the pulsating pain didn't hurt as much as her feelings inside.

I want to be with him, a voice inside Maren said.

Maren shook her head. *Nonsense*, she called herself to order. *He's not much different from his twin. Just less obvious. You are a goose to fall for him. A stupid goose.*

I could lean against him. He's quite close, and he might think it's only because of the pain.

Stop it! You've learned the hard way it's better to rely on yourself. Stick to it, and you'll be fine.

"I'll go and drive my car to the end of the pier," he said. "Then I'll come back to help you."

"Don't bother," Maren scowled at him so he would see she meant it. "As I said, I'll take my car home."

He lifted his eyebrows. "Oh, yeah? Show me how you'll walk to the end of the pier, then."

Maren scrambled to her feet. She clenched her teeth and lifted her chin, but the second she put weight on her right foot, she pitched forward.

He caught her. Her nose pressed against his shirt. She smelled his aftershave and heard his voice in her hair.

"Stubborn, aren't you?"

"Hmmph." Maren struggled up and he released her immediately, but kept ahold of her arm so she wouldn't fall. She started to hop but the pier seemed to have gotten two miles longer. By the time they reached his car, she was shaking and close to tears. With a suppressed sigh, she sank into the passenger's seat and closed her eyes. When she opened them again, he leaned against the open door and watched her.

Maren swallowed. "Thanks." She tried to make her voice stable. "Okay, so I won't take my car tonight. Could you drive me home, please?"

He smiled down at her. "I will. Right after Poulsbo." He closed the door, went around the car, and climbed inside.

Maren said, "I don't think they have emergency service at Poulsbo. Besides, I don't need to go. A little ice will do."

"I'm sorry to stifle your optimism, but it won't." He started the BMW.

"I thought you were a tax consultant, not a doctor." She didn't want to sound rude, but she had no time to be ill. She had to drive her car. She had to visit her customers. She had to drive Sherry to . . .

He threw her a look and smiled. "I spent my teenage years playing baseball, and I've seen quite a few sprained ankles. If it swells like that, it should be seen to by a doctor."

His smile did strange things to her breathing. She saw understanding in it, mixed with compassion, and it unsettled her. She needed to put some distance between them. Now. If the pain continued to cloud her brain and make her shaky and dependent, she'd topple into his arms sooner or later.

She didn't want that.

Yes, she did.

Oh, no!

Anything might happen with her brain fuzzy from pain. "I need to go home."

"Maren," he said. "I promise to take you home right afterward. Are you afraid of doctors?"

"No."

"Then what is it?" He turned onto Winslow Way.

I'm afraid of you. Or rather, me. She clenched her hands. Oh, how she wanted to go home, curl up, and cry. But when she looked at the now grotesque shape of her ankle, she knew she'd better follow his advice. Suddenly, she remembered Annie. "I've got a better idea," she said. "Could you take me to Annie?"

"Who's Annie?"

"A dear friend. She lives next to my parents' house, and she's a doctor."

"Does she have X-ray equipment in her living room?"

"Very funny. But still, I would prefer to go to Annie. She lives just around the corner, and we wouldn't have to drive all the way to Poulsbo. The center might be closed anyway." She slanted him a look. He didn't look convinced. "If it continues to hurt, I can always go to a doctor on Monday."

He frowned and shook his head.

Darn. How to convince him? "Besides, it'll be cheaper." Maybe that would do the trick. He should know the startup of a new company was an expensive thing.

He knew, all right, she could tell by the way he kept his gaze on the road to avoid embarrassing her. "All right. Show me the way."

Maren relaxed. Thank God. If Annie was close— Annie who knew how little she appreciated Chris—she would manage to keep her distance. "She lives on Yeomalt Point Drive. You've got to turn left into Ferncliff Avenue over there."

"Did you see the time?" Tony suddenly asked. "It's almost one in the morning. Are you sure she'll be awake?"

Chapter Four

Maren swallowed. He was right; it wasn't exactly the right time to pay a social call. But as they turned into the drive, she saw light spilling through the open windows and heard a melody floating across the wild flowers that were Annie's idea of a lawn.

Annie opened the door, and her voluminous lilac dress floated out like a cloud. Maren hopped forward, with Tony's hand under her elbow. "I'm sorry to disturb you, Annie."

Annie grasped the situation with a glance and started to laugh. "Welcome, dear," she said. "It'll be quite a family meeting." She opened the door wide and revealed Maren's father and mother sitting in the living room.

Maren wanted to disappear into thin air. She saw her mother exchange a startled glance with her father and knew they would never believe the story of a business meeting that ended at one a.m. She clenched her teeth. "Hi, Mom, Dad. I turned my ankle and thought Annie might put something on it. Oh, this is . . . Chris Mountforth from Mountforth and Adams."

As Tony shook hands with her parents, Annie towed Maren toward the sofa and examined the ankle. "You'll have to get an X-ray," she said. "Just to make sure nothing's broken."

Maren threw a glance at Tony, who tried in vain to suppress a twinkle in his blue-green eyes.

"Oh, has she refused to go to the emergency center?" Maren's father asked. "She's a little stubborn at times."

"I know." Tony smiled at Maren in a way that made her heart gallop. What on earth was he doing? He couldn't smile like that when her father and mother were watching! They'd get the wrong idea altogether. His dark hair was still ruffled from the wind, and there was something about the set of his shoulders that made her want to lean against him.

Her father said, "I know your father, Chris. He's a great golfer and proud to have you in the company."

Tony and Maren both winced.

Annie shot a look from one to the other and said, "I'll get some ointment and a bandage for your ankle, Maren."

"Thanks." Maren dropped back into the cushions and closed her eyes. Maybe she could imagine herself away. The evening was getting too complicated.

"Poor thing," her mother said. "How did it happen?"

"She caught her heel on the edge of the pier as we got out of the boat," Tony said.

Maren knew without opening her eyes that her mother shook her head. "I've told her time and again she shouldn't put on such silly shoes."

Great. Maren felt like a five-year-old. All in front of a gorgeous-looking man who was masquerading to be her business partner. Couldn't she disappear into a mouse hole somewhere?

"I wouldn't blame the shoes. It's a tricky edge. I stumbled myself at that point last week," Tony said.

Her eyes flew open and looked directly into his laughing ones. Maren swallowed. Not only gorgeous but kind. His brother would have told her parents her shoes were sexy.

Annie came back and bandaged the foot. It took all of Maren's self-control not to grab a cushion and bite into it.

"Done." Annie scrutinized her face. "You're a bit pale, my dear. I'll get you some tea and a pain killer."

"No pain killer," Maren said. "I had a glass of wine during dinner."

Annie frowned. "Right. Just the herbal tea, then."

Maren shuddered. Annie's herbal teas tasted like dried grass with a few forgotten grasshoppers.

Annie brought the tea and a glass with something else for Tony, and before Maren knew what was happening, they sat in a cozy round as if Tony had been part of the family for ages. It should have felt strange and unreal. Instead, it felt good. Her parents discussed every restaurant on Bainbridge Island and the Greater Puget Sound Area with Tony. Annie listened and watched with a smile. From time to time, she threw a puzzled glance from Maren to Tony.

Oh, no. Maren knew what she was thinking. Annie was trying to reconcile the man to the story she had heard earlier.

Maren's eyelids felt heavy as she sank deeper into the cushions. The sofa was so comfortable. She'd spent a few nights here as a child, when her parents had been away. Did the herbal tea make her drowsy?

She heard her father say, "Well, Chris, as you're here, I might just as well ask you a little question I've been wanting to discuss with your father. You see, I got an appraisal for the property tax that—"

Maren shot up. "Dad! You can't ask Chris to discuss taxes in the middle of the night."

Annie lifted her eyebrows and shot a look from Maren to Tony.

Maren's father looked like a sheep. "I'm sorry," he said. "Maren's right, of course."

Tony shook his head. "That's not a problem, but actually, it's best if you talk to my father. He'll be able to give you the best advice as he knows your entire dossier. I will tell him to call you first thing on Monday morning."

Maren stared at her empty glass. What on earth had come over her? By rights, she should have enjoyed watching Tony squirm. Instead, she saved him. Why? Out of the corner of her eyes, she threw a look at him. He stared at her. Hastily, she turned her head and said, "Dad, why don't you tell T . . . em, Chris, how we came to live on Bainbridge Island?" She knew her father loved to recite the story of his life. It would keep him busy for at least half an hour, and it was a good method to avoid hot topics. As her father talked and Tony listened, Maren's mother slipped her chair closer and said in a low voice, "He's nice, your young man."

"He's not my young man." Maren clenched her teeth. "He's a business partner."

"And good-looking too."

Maren balled her fists. She was not going to scream. She would keep cool and aloof. As she opened her eyes again, she met Tony's. His face was bent toward her father as if there was nothing more interesting than the story, but his laughing eyes teased her. He must have understood. Maren felt the blood well up in her face.

Her mother smiled. "I'm sure Sherry will get along with him just fine."

Maren felt the hairs on the back of her neck rise. "My foot hurts." She laid back and closed her eyes. She would pretend to sleep. Let them sort it out. She'd had it up to the limit.

A hand shook his shoulder. "Come on, Chris, wake up!"

"One more sec, baby." Chris turned around. His limbs

felt heavy, and his eyes burned as if someone had rubbed grit into them.

"I'm not your baby, and you'd better wake up now."

He knew that voice. Chris opened one eye and stared into the bright lightbulb of his bedroom. It hurt. "Tony? What do you want?" He lifted his arm and squinted at his wristwatch but his eyes couldn't focus. "It's the middle of the night."

"It's a quarter to three."

Chris groaned and hid his head beneath the cushion. Maybe Tony would go away. Tony pulled the pillow from beneath him, went to the window and flung it wide open. "Come on, wake up. I need to talk to you."

"Now?" Chris groaned again. His tongue felt furry.

"Now."

"I've only been in bed for half an hour or so. Kitty's computer crashed completely."

Chris groped for a bottle of Coke beneath his bed, opened it, and took a deep swig. It ran down his throat cool and sweet. "That's better." With a sigh, he sat up and faced his brother. "What's so urgent it can't wait?" He rubbed his eyes, but when he remembered their switched roles, he shot up. "Don't tell me anything went wrong with Maren?"

Tony leaned against his wardrobe. "We have to tell Maren the truth tomorrow—I mean today."

Chris felt as if someone had emptied a bucked with icy water over him. "What?"

"You heard me."

"But that's crazy! I take it she hasn't guessed?"

"I . . . I'm not sure."

Chris took a deep breath. "Gosh, you scared me." He frowned. "But if she hasn't guessed, we'd be stupid to tell her. You just tell me all I need to know, and we'll take it from there." A smile spread over his face. "Why, you never need to see her again."

"That's just the problem," Tony said.

Chris narrowed his eyes. Was Tony drunk? "What do you mean?"

"I very much intend to see her again."

"You . . ." Chris shook his head, but when the words registered, he froze and his mouth dropped open. "You're not telling me you . . . you like her? Maren Christensen?'

"Is that her last name?" Tony tilted his head to one side. "Yes, you said her family is Swedish, didn't you? You know, it suits her. Kind of Nordic."

"Kind of glacial, rather!" Chris rubbed his face. Had Tony gone mad? "Come on, admit you're kidding me. You can't be serious."

Tony didn't reply.

"Tony, stop teasing me."

Tony smiled. A strange smile, a smile Chris had never seen before. It scared him. "Tell me the truth, now. What's the game you're playing?"

"I'm not playing a game. It's probably the most serious thing I've done in a long time."

Chris didn't move. Granted, Tony had been on a rather conservative trip recently, but making up to Maren was crazy. He eyed his twin. "Listen, brother, you're making a mistake. Maybe she took you in tonight." He frowned and tried to recall the start of the evening. "I admit she looked quite nice in that dress, and she does have those stunning ankles, but she's about as comfortable as a tiger. You never know when she'll spring at you next. And she's darn serious."

Tony's smile made Chris want to throw the Coke at him. "If you tell her the truth, she'll eat your head off. And what's more, mine too."

Tony nodded. "I know. But there's no alternative."

Darn. Chris knew that tone. He jumped up and took his brother by the shoulders. "Why stir up muddy waters? We can find a better solution! I can introduce you sometime next week. You invite her out. Why destroy everything?"

Finally, he seemed to get through. Tony stared at him with a frown. Chris pushed his advantage. "It'll be better for her. Just think how humiliating it would be if we told her we'd fooled her."

He regretted the words the moment they were out of his mouth.

Tony pressed his lips into one straight line. "No." His voice sounded as if it was made of concrete.

Chris grabbed the bottle of Coke and took another swig. "Why not?"

Tony seemed to search for words. "I can't base our relationship on a lie."

Chris leaned against the windowsill, bottle still in hand. How on earth could he beat some sense into that man? "Listen, bro. I know Maren. I know her well. She'll dissect you. You won't get a chance to base any kind of relationship on anything at all if you tell her the truth. Have you considered that?"

Tony hesitated. "I told you, she might have guessed already."

Chris bent forward to push his advantage, but the soda bottle slipped from his grasp. The brown liquid washed over the wooden floor and spread like a lake with a broken dam. "What a mess!" Chris looked around for something to mop it up. "You're not making any sense, you know. Pass me that black T-shirt over there. If she guessed, why do we need to tell her?"

"Here." Tony handed the shirt to him. "Because I need to clear it up. You won't have to say anything. Just come with me. I'll do the talking. You know, you should use some water. It'll get all sticky."

"What?" Chris blinked. "Oh, you mean the Coke. Yes, I'll do that tomorrow." He dropped back onto his bed and stared at his brother. "I can't believe you're that gone on her. Just what happened tonight?"

Tony's cheeks reddened.

Chris whistled. "Don't tell me you . . . ?"

Tony grinned. "I took her for a midnight cruise. Later, we met her parents and an old friend of the family. It was quite jolly. I didn't kiss her good night, if that's what you want to know."

"I don't believe it."

"Gosh, Chris, stop behaving as if she's a woman from Mars!"

"For all I know she may be."

"No, she is not," Tony's eyes narrowed. "Oh, she's cool and controlled and efficient, I'll grant you that. But underneath, she's also . . ." He stopped and stared at his hands, ". . . different."

"I have to take your word for it." Chris wondered if he had strayed into a bad dream. He pinched himself, but Tony still looked infatuated. Maren and Tony? It was preposterous. "Can you tell me why she should all of a sudden be different tonight of all nights?"

Tony smiled. "Of course I can. Because I'm not like you."

"I see. That makes it crystal clear." He wanted to sling the soaked T-shirt into his brother's face to wipe away that grin.

Tony shook his head. "Chris, I know you don't understand. You don't have to. Just help me clear up this mess. Come with me, and let's tell her the truth. For the rest, I'll take responsibility."

Chris clenched his teeth. Tony seldom turned stubborn, but if he did, there was no stopping him. Darn his overactive conscience.

He had to try another tactic. Chris leaned his back against the wall and watched his brother beneath half-closed lids. "Okay. Since you introduced conditions, I'll make one too. You'll forget the stuff about changing jobs, and I'll talk to her."

Tony interrupted him. "No way. I deceived her; I need to tell her. Besides, I won't forget my condition."

Chris wanted to throttle him. "Why on earth do you insist I quit? You know," he forced a laugh, "it seems as if you're jealous that I work with Dad and you don't."

Tony pushed himself away from the wardrobe. His voice sounded quiet and controlled, but Chris wasn't fooled. "It'll hurt you and Dad if you continue."

"Only if you walk around telling everybody our secrets."

"Listen, Chris. She tried to talk business tonight, and . . . you have to make an effort if you want to keep her as a client."

Chris rolled his eyes. "Oh, no. Of course she had to talk about work. I've never seen anyone so uptight. Can she never relax?"

Tony narrowed his eyes. "You don't get it, do you?"

Chris shrugged. "Some people know how to live. Others know how to work. What did you say when she started with her job-talk?"

"I turned her off. But you'd better get in touch with her next week. Something about Jill Spencer's contract and the Smith documents."

Chris rubbed his forehead. "I don't know anything about any Smith documents."

"Of course not." Tony's irony cut through him.

Chris felt anger welling up inside him. "And whatever they may be when they're at home, I'm not willing to discuss business at three in the morning."

Tony shook his head. "Your enthusiasm floors me."

Chris swallowed. They used to be friends. They could rely on each other, always. And now? Now his brother had turned into a stranger. A supercilious, conservative, stupid stranger. Chris couldn't bear him anymore. He flung the T-shirt to the floor. "Get out, Tony. I want to sleep."

Tony didn't budge. "I want to tell Maren the truth."

Chris glared at his twin. It was incredible. Did nothing get through to him? "Ever heard the word loyalty, Tony?" He bent forward and clenched his hands. "Listen, brother, and listen well. Whatever happens, I want you to know one thing: If you breathe one word to Maren, we're through. Got that?" He angled for his pillow on the floor, threw it onto his bed, pummeled it into shape, dropped onto it, then turned his back on Tony and covered his head with his bedspread. His ex-brother could find his own way out. What a rotten, rotten night.

When Maren woke up, the sun was shining into Annie's living room. Her foot throbbed, and her tongue felt furry, but at least her head was clear. For a minute, she didn't move and tried to recall every minute of last night. Had it been a dream? A nightmare, rather?

She stared at her ankle. That part, at least, was real. Then the rest had to be true as well. Had she fallen for

Chris' brother? Impossible. The Mountforth kind of charm was not her cup of tea at all.

A rustle made her turn her head. Annie peeped around the corner. "Oh, you're awake." She marched into the room with tinkling earrings and put her head to one side while searching Maren's face. "How's the foot?"

"Throbbing."

"Hmm. Maybe Chris should take you to the emergency center today."

Maren shot up. "Chris? What do you mean? Is he still here?"

Annie grinned. "Oh, no. But he promised to be back for breakfast, with fresh cinnamon rolls." She glanced at her lilac watch. "He'll arrive in twenty minutes."

Maren swallowed. "Just what exactly happened last night?"

"After you fell asleep, you mean?"

Maren nodded.

"Well, your father and Chris compared life on Bainbridge Island to every other island in the world and concluded it beat them all."

Maren sighed. "And now they're friends for evermore."

"Exactly. Your mother seemed happy enough to plan your wedding."

Maren's head shot up. "What?"

Annie grinned. "Well, no, she didn't. But she took to him in a great way."

"She would take to any man because she thinks that with Sherry, I'll never find one." Maren bit her lips.

"I think you're a bit unjust there. He looked at you as you were asleep, and his face softened with tenderness."

"Ha. His face only softened because he tried to hide his grin."

Annie shook her head. "Certainly not. By the way, I could see the charm you described to me, but I failed to discover the eel qualities you mentioned."

Maren stared at her hands and didn't reply. Should she tell Annie? She couldn't bring herself to confess how the twins had fooled her. Why had Tony promised to come back? Would he send Chris instead? She shuddered. Maybe he wouldn't show up at all and call with a flimsy excuse. "Annie, who came up with the idea of sharing breakfast?"

"Hmm . . . let me see. I'm not sure. The cinnamon rolls were my idea. But I think he started to talk about breakfast."

That didn't help. Maren placed her feet with care onto the floor. "Would you help me hop to the bathroom? If he shows up, I don't want to face him with yesterday's makeup."

"Sure." Annie took her arm. "By the way, I've got to go in five minutes. I've promised my mother I'd come over."

"What?" Maren stared at her. "But . . . Chris will come and . . ."

"Oh." Annie grinned. "I don't think you'll miss me."

Maren was speechless. Perfect. Breakfast with Chris or Tony or whoever would come. And she was still in her clothes from yesterday. Maybe Annie could lend her something.

Then again, no. It was certain to be billowy and lilac, and she would look like something leftover from the sixties. Gosh. Could it be she was nervous just because one of the Mountforth twins wanted to come for breakfast? She didn't recognize herself.

Chapter Five

Tony left the bakery with the bag of cinnamon rolls in his left hand. He hummed and skipped down the two steps that led to the sidewalk. The sky was hazy blue and arched promisingly over Bainbridge Island. He had no idea what he would tell Maren, but the thought of seeing her made his blood tingle.

His cell phone rang. Could it be Maren? He shook his head. How could he be so infatuated? She didn't even have his number.

"Tony Mountforth speaking."

"Mr. Mountforth? This is the Northwest Hospital in Seattle." The female voice sounded like a computer.

Tony stopped in his tracks. Something cold gripped his stomach. "Yes?"

"We've got a Guiseppe Maglia here with an acute case of appendicitis. He wants you to come."

"Guiseppe?" Tony clutched the bag with a cold hand. Pictures tumbled through his mind. Guiseppe at his job interview seven years ago, his curls flattened by mousse. Guiseppe, welcoming their regular guests with outstretched arms, a smile stretching from ear to ear. Guiseppe with a triumphant grin after the first night they were fully booked. Guiseppe with shiny eyes, telling him about the birth of his first child. "How bad is it?"

"We wanted to operate on him already, but he insists he must speak to you first. How soon can you be here?"

Tony swallowed. "The ferry . . ." He checked his watch. "I believe I can catch the one in fifteen minutes."

"Good. Hurry."

Tony jumped into his car and raced to the ferry. He felt dumb and cold. Guiseppe. If they wanted to operate on him Saturday morning, it was bad. Nobody died nowadays because of appendicitis, did they? He had no clue. What about Rosalie and the kids? Were they with him?

A thought rushed through him like a flame. Maren. He was supposed to have breakfast with Maren. Tony closed his eyes. He had to call her. He could explain that his chef, his closest employee and friend who had stood next to him in all the ups and downs of the beginning, had to be operated on and—he stopped dead.

He couldn't tell her anything. She thought he was

Chris. And Chris didn't have a chef. Should he say somebody else got ill, somebody Chris knew? But where would that lead? Besides, she wouldn't care. He hit the steering wheel with his flat hand and accelerated too much on the ramp, which brought him a warning shout from the ferry clerk.

What to do? He could think of just one alternative, and it made him wince, but he couldn't disappoint Maren yet again. How many times had Chris made her wait in vain? Three? He was not going to add a fourth time.

He stopped the motor and whipped out his cell phone. As he entered Chris' number he prayed his brother would answer the phone.

Chris answered on the fifth ring. "What do you want now?"

"I need your help, Chris. I've promised Maren we would have breakfast at ten but I need to go and see Guiseppe at the hospital. He's got appendicitis. Can you go and take my place?"

"What? You want me to have breakfast with the iceberg?"

"She's not an iceberg!"

"Why on earth did you set up a second date?"

"Chris." Tony clenched his teeth. "Will you or won't you go?"

"Why does Guiseppe want you? He's got his wife . . . what's her name again?"

"Rosalie. I have no clue why he insists on seeing me.

But if the hospital calls me and says I've got to come presto, I don't argue."

Chris sighed. "Okay, okay, I'll go. But if she bites my head off, you know who's responsible."

"Man, you're famous for your charm. Use it! And make sure you're on time." Tony hung up. He had betrayed Maren. With a sick feeling, he waited for the ferry to arrive in Seattle.

"Tell me everything." Tony clamped the phone between his shoulder and his head and polished the glass in his hands without seeing it.

"Hello to you too." Chris sounded tired. "How is Guiseppe?"

"The operation went fine. I'll drive back to Seattle to collect Rosalie later in the evening. Did you see Maren?" Tony hung the glass upside down onto the rack and took the next.

"Why did Guiseppe insist to see you?" Chris asked.

Darn Chris. Couldn't he reply to a question? "He made me promise I would take care of Rosalie and the kids if the operation turned out bad." For an instant, Tony saw Guiseppe's eyes again, full of fear.

"It wasn't a heart operation, just a bit of appendicitis, was it?"

Tony clenched his teeth. "You've never been afraid of anything, have you?"

Chris sighed. "Yes. I'm afraid of your iceberg."

Tony's hands stilled. "Did you go?"

"Of course I went. I promised to, didn't I?"

Tony resumed the polishing. "Thanks. What did she say?"

"She looked at me . . . let me see . . . as if I were a snail on a piece of lettuce and asked where I left the cinnamon rolls."

"Darn. I forgot. They're still in my car."

"Thanks, bro. I did look kind of foolish and admitted I had forgotten them in my haste to be in her presence."

Tony winced but didn't say anything. "And then?"

"And then she said without cinnamon rolls there was no point in having breakfast, and she made me drive her home."

This was worse than he'd thought. "She didn't even offer you coffee?"

"Oh, she did. With as much enthusiasm as if I had been Jack the Ripper."

Tony sighed. "Between the two of us, we've made it as bad as it could get."

"I'm sorry, I had nothing to do with it. You invited yourself to breakfast, and you asked me to cover for you."

Tony sighed. "Yeah, yeah." He lifted the glass against the light to check if it was clean.

"By the way, you forgot to tell me how she turned her ankle."

Tony closed his eyes. "I hope you didn't ask?"

"I recalled just in time that it might have happened while you were with her."

Tony started breathing again. "Thank God. Sorry."

"She told me it hurt much less . . ."

"Good."

". . . and managed to make me feel bad I hadn't asked."

"Hmph."

"Where are you?"

"At work. Where else?"

"Don't pretend you don't like it. You wanted it that way."

"I know." Tony felt like throwing a glass onto the floor.

"Oh, by the way," Chris said, "I'm not going to quit working for Dad. I figure we're even now, after my breakfast with the iceberg."

"Chris . . ."

"No."

Tony sighed. "At least drop Maren's account."

"Why should I?"

"Because you two don't get along."

"Well, now that you mention it, I think that's a good idea. I'll talk to Dad about it."

When Tony hung up, he felt drained, like a wrung-out dishcloth. He would have to work for two in the next weeks until Guiseppe was back. He didn't have a moment to spare. And yet, his thoughts returned to Maren as if magnetized. He wanted to see her. The feeling was so strong, it felt like a physical ache. But the chances that she would agree to see him were nil. On second thought, maybe she would come—to punch him in the face.

Later in the evening, Tony drove once again to Northwest Hospital and collected Rosalie. Guiseppe was already out of intensive care and gripped Tony's hand in a way that brought tears to his eyes. "Hey, you're breaking my hand. Shall I take Rosalie home now?"

"*Sì.*" Guiseppe inclined his head with caution, a far cry from his usual vigorous nod that shook his whole body. "*Grazie,* Tony."

It happened as they drove off the ferry. Tony's van crept past the cars waiting to get onto the ferry, and Tony's gaze swept over them without interest when he discovered Maren. She sat next to her father in a blue pickup and looked straight at him, then at Rosalie.

Tony froze. The next instant, they had rolled past. Rosalie chattered on, never noticing how quiet Tony had become all of a sudden.

Maren hissed under her breath. It had been Tony! And who was the dark woman next to him? An attractive woman too! Tony had met her eyes and pretended not to know her. How dare he? These stupid, stupid brothers, making fun of her, playing with her. Maren curled her fingers. Oh, if she could get her hands around Tony's neck and wring it.

"Everything all right, dear?" her father said with a sidelong glance.

Maren drew herself up. "Sure. Why do you ask?"

"I thought you made some funny noise, as if you were short of breath."

Maren swallowed. "No. No, I'm fine, Dad."

"Wasn't that Chris Mountforth in the car just now?"

"No, it . . ." Maren stopped herself just in time. "Um, I . . . I didn't see him."

"You know, I'm glad you're going out with him. He's a nice man, and you deserve one."

Maren hunched her shoulders. "I'm not going out with him, Dad." *And I wouldn't go out with either of these darn twins if I got money for it! Big money.*

Her father smiled. "Well, whatever it is you call it nowadays. I guess I'm too old to understand."

Maren closed her eyes.

"His father always tells me how proud he is to have him in the family business. It seems his younger son is somewhat of a disappointment to him and . . ."

"Magnus Mountforth is rather dense if he doesn't see that the younger is by far the better." Maren almost spat out the sentence. "He built up a business all on his own whereas Chris can do nothing but reap profit of the business his father built up!" *Oh, no!* Maren slapped her hand in front of her mouth. What on earth had come over her? Why should she try to defend Tony—Tony who didn't matter one iota to her? "Sorry, Dad. I didn't want to insult your friend."

Her father shot her a troubled look. "It's all right, dear. Though I admit I don't understand . . ." He stopped talking and frowned at the street ahead.

Maren didn't offer to explain. It was all too complicated anyway.

Tony tried to get her out of his head. It should have been easy. With Guiseppe in the hospital, he had to work extra shifts and could only go home to his apartment whenever his eyes threatened to close of their own will. But nothing helped. Whenever a woman with chestnut hair entered his restaurant, his heart stopped for an instant. Whenever he saw a broad mouth, a pang of longing stabbed him. In a weak moment, he even told Guiseppe about her when he went to see him in the hospital. He didn't say much, just that he'd met a woman he couldn't forget.

By the beginning of the third week, Guiseppe had come back, and Tony's workload got lighter, but his curious longing didn't go away. Tony wiped the tables in the kitchen with more vigor than necessary, wishing he could wipe out his memory in the same way. "It's crazy. I've only met her once, and I can't get her out of my mind."

"Eh?" Guiseppe put a bowl with dough onto the table and grinned. He was still pale and thinner than before the operation. "You still thinking about that Maren?"

"Mm-hmm." Tony took the dough out of the bowl and started to roll it into a flat shape.

"Hey, that's my job." Guiseppe frowned.

"You sit down and relax," Tony said. "Making pasta is hard work." He flashed a grin at his friend. "Or so

you always say. That's why I'll do it for once. It was
stupid to offer homemade ramson pasta as a special this
week. We should have taken something easy. Like homemade soup."

Guiseppe pulled a chair close and dropped on to it.
Tony threw him a look. It was a bad sign if Guiseppe
obeyed without protest. He would have to insist on
sending him home sooner tonight.

Guiseppe folded his hands in front of his stomach
and stretched out his legs. "You still thinking about that
woman?" he said once again.

"Yeah." Tony wondered if he had been right to confide in him.

"So tell me," Guiseppe grinned. "What's so special?
She's beautiful, eh?"

Tony shook his head. "No. I mean, yes, of course
she's beautiful. But that's not it."

"No, no? She has nice legs?"

Tony slapped the dough with his flat hand. "She has
nice ankles," he said, "but that's not it either."

"So." Guiseppe leaned his head against the back of
the chair. "You tell me."

Tony frowned at the dough and pummeled the edges
into shape. "She . . . she's sharp."

"Sharp?" Guiseppe jerked. "What you mean, sharp?
Like a knife?"

"No. She's clever. Intelligent. Works hard."

"Hmm." Guiseppe looked as if Tony had lost his
mind. "But is she gentle? Kind?"

A silent laugh shook Tony. "No. No, I wouldn't say she's gentle, as a rule. She can be quite tough when crossed."

"Tony, you better keep your distance," Guiseppe said with a worried look. "A sharp woman who's not kind doesn't sound good. No, not at all."

Tony thought about Rosalie, then compared her to Maren. They were as similar as a kitten to a tiger. But still . . . he couldn't analyze it, couldn't explain, but something had happened that evening, something he tried to fight, but it proved to be stronger.

For the tenth time that day, he wondered if he should ask Chris to engineer a meeting. But he hadn't heard from Chris ever since that Sunday. His brother was probably still mad at him because he'd forgotten to mention the cinnamon rolls. Tony sighed.

The phone rang. Tony suppressed an oath. Of course it always rang when he was up to the elbows in flour. He cleaned his hands and grabbed the receiver. "Tony's restaurant, how can I help you?"

A man's voice answered. "Could I talk to Tony Mountforth, please?"

"Speaking."

"Hello, Mr. Mountforth. Craigh Brown here, of the Washington Culinary Institute in Seattle."

Tony lifted his eyebrows. Craigh Brown, the director of the WCI? A picture jumped into his mind. Mr. Brown, fluffy hair illuminated by the lights behind him, handing him his diploma at the graduation ceremony some eight years ago. What on earth did he want? "What can I do for you, Mr. Brown?"

"We've followed your progress with pleasure, and we're proud that one of our former students receives such outstanding praise. The latest ranking of Tony's Restaurant in the Seattle Restaurant List has made us wonder whether you'd like to come tell our students about your career."

Tony blinked. Mr. Brown was known for never wasting his words, but this was a bit sudden. Had he heard him correctly? He swallowed. "Well, I . . . I'm honored, of course. What exactly did you have in mind?"

"We thought we might group our classes together one morning and you'd come as a visitor to address them all at once. Maybe you remember; it's a kind of tradition on the last day before we close for the summer vacation."

Tony swallowed. What on earth should he tell them? "I see. And I should tell your students about . . . er, about what?"

"Well, everything. How you decided to open the restaurant, about the obstacles, about the things to consider when starting your business, and so on."

The last words rang a bell inside Tony's head. He brought himself up short. That was it!

"I've just had an idea, Mr. Brown." His voice sounded squeaky, and he hastened to lower it. "I have an acquaintance who specializes in consulting for new businesses. Perhaps we could make a combined class, where I tell the students about the practical side, and my acquaintance gives all the up-to-date business background?"

"Hmm." Tony could hear a clink as if something metallic had touched the receiver. In spite of his nervousness, he had to smile. Mr. Owl, the students had called him. No wonder. He was plump, his wisps of hair looked feathery, and his thick glasses made it easy to see a likeness. They had often imitated the way he kept taking down his glasses and polishing them before answering a question. "Well." It sounded as if Mr. Brown had some more polishing to do before he could make a decision. Tony heard him clearing his throat, "It's difficult to decide without knowing her. Why don't you come and present your idea to me together, and then we'll see if we can fit it in?"

A flutter unsettled Tony's stomach. "I'll talk to her about it."

He hung up and turned to Guiseppe, who had continued to work on the pasta as soon as Tony had turned his back. "I've got it! And you have to stop working on the dough right now."

"You got what?"

"I've found a way to get in touch with Maren!"

Guiseppe shook his head. "There's no fool like a man in love," he said. "But at least I have finished the pasta."

The next hour, Tony prepared for the all-important call by practicing different ways to speak on the phone. Finally, he closed the door to his office, wrote his sentences with clammy hands, and keyed her number into his phone.

Chapter Six

Every morning when Maren opened her eyes, she saw his face. It wasn't fair. She had taken away his card from her mirror and hidden it deep inside her drawer, but it hadn't helped.

Even her bandaged foot reminded her of Tony. At first, she had needed a crutch, but it was better now. If only everything healed as well as a foot. She sighed. How she hated his guts. She hated him and his supercilious brother. She hated them ever since Chris had turned into Annie's drive that awful morning. She'd felt double-cheated. If it had been Tony, she might have . . . *No, no. Don't even think about it, girl.*

Only one thing had given her some satisfaction in the last two weeks . . . the interview with her new tax consultant. Susan Catterick had set up her company two years ago and still knew how it felt to be with one's back to the wall. More to the point, she was eager, sharp, and knowledgeable. It was a pleasure to break with Mountforth and Adams, even though they might not know it yet. But otherwise, life had lost its sparkle and reminded her of old chewing gum—gray and disgusting.

When the phone rang, Maren jumped and threw a look at the clock on the wall. It was her mother's time. If only she wouldn't mention the oh-so-wonderful Mountforth twins. Then again, maybe she was lucky, and it was Henry Barker Productions. You never knew.

"The Start-Up Company, Maren Christensen speaking."

"Hi, this is Tony Mountforth."

Maren's mouth dropped open. She tried to make a sound, but nothing came out.

"Ms. Christensen? Are you there?"

What did he call her? Ms. Christensen? Was he going to pretend he didn't know her? Would he dare to continue with the masquerade? Maren pulled herself together. "Er. Yes." Her voice sounded as if she had a sore throat.

"My brother told me you consult for people who want to start up a new business."

Oh, no. He *was* pretending not to know her. How rotten. And trying to talk business. She had to keep her wits. "Yes." Her voice sounded worse by the minute.

"As you may know, I founded my restaurant called Tony's here on Bainbridge Island seven years ago. I've just had an offer from the culinary school in Seattle where I used to be a student. They want me to come and give a talk to the students."

"Ah." If she continued with grunts, he would hang up in a minute. "Yes?" Great. That made a true change. He would think she was a nitwit.

"And I thought it might be good if we did a speech together."

"What?" Maren couldn't help it, she shouted the word.

"Yes, I know it seems strange, but I thought we might turn it into something brilliant. You would give the facts and the general information about starting up a restaurant, and I would illustrate it with my example and tell a few anecdotes."

She could well imagine it. He would dish out funny stories, ladled with the Mountforth charm, and whenever it was her turn, the audience would fall asleep. She didn't want to work with him. She couldn't. She didn't want to be close to him. Oh, yes, she wanted to. But not to work. She wanted to . . . Maren shook herself. "Ah," she said.

"I know it's a bit sudden. Couldn't we meet somewhere and discuss it?"

Before Maren could stop to think, she heard herself shout "No!"

"I beg your pardon?" Tony seemed startled.

"I'm sorry, I'm—er—a mosquito just bit me. Er—yes. I—listen, I'll have to think about it. Can you give me your number, and I'll call you back?"

"Yes, certainly."

He gave her his business and cell phone number. As soon as he said good-bye, the receiver dropped from Maren's hand as if it were too heavy to hold. Maren stared at it. Had she dreamed the call? She felt numb. As if on autopilot, she got up, drained a huge glass of water, tore open a bag of gummy bears, fished out a white bear, and chewed it with fierce determination. What should she do?

Maren struggled to take a deep breath. She would set Tony's project aside and think about it in a few hours. By then, she would have calmed down. Yes, time was all it took.

The back door banged and Sherry darted in. "Mommy! I'm home!"

Maren pulled herself together. She looked at her daughter as if seeing her for the first time. How sweet she looked with her pigtails all askew and her shiny blue eyes. Maren's heart constricted. Nothing mattered but Sherry's happiness. "Hi, darling. How was school?"

"Cool."

Maren smiled. How long would it take before Sherry pretended school bored her? She was glad that Sherry still liked it, after almost one year.

"Do you want to bake a cake with me, darling?" Maybe it would take her mind off Tony. It was a good way to reduce stress. Usually, it worked, but she had a gloomy feeling that Tony's project might prove to be cake-resistant.

"Yes!" Sherry dropped her jacket, bag, and shoes.

Maren pointed at them with raised eyebrows. Sherry collected her jacket again with a pout belied by a mischievous glance out of the corner of her eyes, and hung it on the yellow peg beside the door, then put the other things away.

Maren opened the fridge and took out the butter. In disbelief, she stared at the new package. Row upon row of tiny holes decorated its surface, punched through the shiny wrap. "Sherry! What on earth is that?" Maren lifted the butter.

Sherry hopped closer, her eyes wide and innocent. "Oh," she said. "I didn't do that! Maybe the Little Ghost?"

Maren caught her hand and put Sherry's index finger into one of holes. It fit perfectly.

"I see," she said. "Just why did you do that?"

"Don't you think it looks nice?"

"No. Not at all."

"But, Mommy, at Carol's party, her mother decorated the butter too, she made loads of little marks on the butter, with the end of her knife, and I thought it was so cool!"

Maren sighed. "The next time you feel like decorating something, use your modeling clay." She bent forward and peered into the fridge. "By the way, is the last batch still on the ceiling?"

Sherry looked at the red lump of clay right above the entrance. "Um. Yes."

Maren suppressed a smile and took out the orange juice, then poured it into a measuring cup.

"Mom!"

"Yes?"

"That's orange juice, not milk!"

Maren stared at the bottle in her hand. "Oh."

Sherry collapsed in giggles.

"I was far away in my thoughts, you see." Maren tried to steady her hands.

"Somewhere nice, Mommy?"

"Hmm. I don't know."

Later, when Sherry was fast asleep, Maren dropped into her favorite chair in the living room and put up her foot to ease the pain she still felt after a day of running around. She leaned back, closed her eyes, and tried to relax. It didn't help. She felt just as wobbly as before whenever she thought about Tony Mountforth and his extraordinary idea.

"Okay, my girl." She discovered a bag with gummy bears on the low table next to her, grabbed a white one, and started to nibble on it. She debated Tony's proposition with herself. "Let's debate this. Imagine it to be Chris instead of Tony. Would you do it?"

"No."

"Why not?"

"Because he wouldn't show up." Maren scratched her head.

"Hmm. Now, imagine he did show up. Would you?"

"No."

"Be honest."

"Well . . ."

"Honest!"

Maren frowned and extracted a piece of gummy bear from between her teeth. "Okay, it's a great opportunity to become better known in Seattle. These students might become clients one day. And they have brothers, sisters, aunts . . . I need every scrap of publicity I can get. Also, the combination of a theoretical and a practical side is a brilliant idea."

"Ha. You won't be able to say a single word with him next to you."

"I'm afraid that's true."

"What? You're supposed to contradict me."

Maren chewed another gummy bear. "If I became a bit used to him, he wouldn't bowl me over anymore."

". . . said the rabbit to the snake before it got hypnotized."

Maren sighed. "You're right of course. On the other hand, it might be a perfect way to take revenge."

"The last revenge was a miserable failure."

"Yeah, well, I'm not used to revenges yet."

"Then better leave your fingers off them."

"Hmmph." Frustrated, Maren bit into a red gummy bear as no white bears were left. "Still . . . I might find an opportunity to get back at him."

"As long as you make sure you don't humiliate yourself in the process. Remember, you have to seem cool and professional."

"Impossible."

"You always pride yourself on being professional. On sticking to the facts. Now here's a job offer. An opportunity for promotion. Don't tell me you want to refuse it just because of some hormones. You're in no position to refuse an offer like that. Think of your daughter."

"You're right."

"Then get it over with before your nerves fail you."

Maren clenched her teeth, grabbed the phone, and punched in Tony's number.

"Tony's Restaurant, you're speaking to Belinda Honor."

Belinda Honor. Who was that? Maren pictured a blond hussy.

"Hi. Maren Christensen here. May I talk to Tony Mountforth?"

"Hold on, please."

An instant later, she heard his voice, cutting right into her. "Ms. Christensen?"

Maren cleared her throat. "Hi. I . . . I'd like to discuss the idea you mentioned earlier today."

It was quiet on the other end of the line. Oh, no. Maybe he had forgotten her already. Maren felt herself break into a cold sweat and babbled on, "You know, the speech at the culinary institute. You said we might do it together." Why didn't he say anything?

It seemed an hour before he answered. "That's great. How about tomorrow morning, say, ten o'clock?"

Maren swallowed. He was quick. She checked her schedule book in front of her. Should she play hard to get? Booked out? No, that would only make her nervous. "Tomorrow would be fine."

"Will you come to the restaurant? We're closed at that time, so we'll have some peace."

"All right. See you tomorrow, then."

When Maren hung up, her hands shook. She had a date with Tony Mountforth.

Tony heard the click in the line. A triumphant grin spread across his face. She had agreed to come. He had not dared to believe it, and when he'd heard her say yes, she'd rendered him speechless.

"Good news?" Belinda asked.

"The best." Tony smiled at her. He turned to go back to the kitchen.

A voice with a Swedish accent said behind him, "Chris Mountforth! What a nice surprise!"

Tony swiveled around and stared straight into the face of Maren's father. *Oh, no.* He was not supposed to know the guy.

Groping for words, he stammered, "Welcome to Tony's restaurant."

Maren's mother beamed at him, and her father opened his mouth, but before he could say something, Tony rushed on, "I'm glad to welcome friends of my brother. I'm not Chris Mountforth, but Tony, his twin." He forced a smile. "People often mistake us."

"Wow, I should think so!" Her father stared at him. "I swear I can't see the tiniest difference!"

No wonder, Tony thought and stretched out his hand to Maren's mother.

"I'm Inga Christensen"—she took his hand—"and this is my husband, Lars."

Tony hoped his forced laugh sounded surprised. "But what a coincidence. I've just talked to your daughter on the phone."

"So you know Maren too?" Inga smiled.

"Not yet. But my brother told me that she's a consultant, and I had an idea we might work together." He had to get off that topic. After all, Maren might only come tomorrow to throw something into his face. "Have you booked a table tonight?"

"No, we just dropped in."

Great. They were fully booked. Tony turned to Belinda and fixed her with a stare. "I believe table three has just been canceled, isn't that right, Belinda?"

Belinda's eyes widened. Table three was one of the most coveted tables due to its view. She looked down at her book of appointments, then up again. "Actually, yes, you're lucky. Will you please come this way, Mrs. and Mr. Christensen?"

Tony heaved a sigh of relief. Well trained. He checked the reservation book, then rearranged them so everybody would fit. Thank God they stuck to their rule of keeping one spare table for emergencies. It had helped them time and again. That was a good piece of advice to pass on to the students. He felt a flutter in his stomach just thinking of it. He hoped Maren would agree to join him.

When the Christensens had finished dinner, he took them both a small glass of Fernet-Branca and sat down at their table. "I hope you enjoyed your meal?"

Inga nodded. "It was wonderful. Lars just said he'd never had such a tender sirloin in his life."

Tony smiled. Whenever he heard a compliment about his restaurant, he felt a warm glow inside, even after all these years. "I'm glad to hear you liked it."

Maren's father cleared his throat. "Actually, I'm happy you came because we've been discussing a problem where you might assist us."

Tony nodded. He would do anything to get into Lars' good books. "Of course, it would be my pleasure."

"I'm going to celebrate my sixtieth birthday in two weeks with a summer party. We have invited all our friends, and I think about fifty people will come." Lars tried in vain to look modest. "However, just this morning we discovered that our caterer went out of business, and we have no clue how to find one on such short notice. Is there anybody you could recommend?"

A family party at the Christensens. If Maren turned up tomorrow just to slap his face, it might offer another chance to meet her. She couldn't throw him out of her father's house, not if he was the emergency caterer. He did a quick inventory of his equipment. It would involve some hard work, but he might borrow a few things from Paul, and . . . yes, it could work. "We don't usually do catering outside our own premises," he said, his mind still busy with the stock, "but seeing as it's so urgent, we might make an exception."

Inga's face glowed. "Oh, that would be perfect!"

But Lars frowned and bit his lips. "There's one hitch, though. I want it to have a Scandinavian theme, as we're from Sweden. I think I told you . . . no, I told your brother. You know, it's amazing how much alike you look."

Tony forced a smile. "Yes, everybody says so."

Lars Christensen nodded. "Well, to come back to Sweden, we emigrated twenty years ago." His accent grew more pronounced. "You can say it was quite a story, how we arrived on Bainbridge Island. In fact, it would never have—"

Tony knew he had to interrupt him before he launched into the story of his life. He leaned forward. "I believe I could make a Swedish buffet, with your help, of course. If you wish, I can get a notepad right now to make a list of all the things you want."

The Christensens were delighted, and half an hour later he had the rough outline for a Swedish summer evening on his pad, including crisp bread with bits of smoked salmon, marinated herring, little meatballs, and princess sponge cake with a marzipan coating. Now he only had to sell the idea to his staff. They would say he was crazy. That didn't bother him. What bothered him was that they weren't far off the mark.

That night was longer than any other night Maren had ever lived through. She tossed and turned, and by the time she was as hot and disgruntled as if she had spent hours hiking through a jungle, she rolled out of bed and padded upstairs to Sherry's room. When she eased open her door, she took a deep breath. The room was filled with Sherry's fragrance; the fragrance that came directly from her skin. Maren smiled. She was addicted to that fragrance, had been from the hour Sherry was born. It soothed her and filled her with a strange happiness. Maren tiptoed closer. Teddy Pimm lay beneath Sherry, one furry ear showing next to her elbow. With care, Maren pulled him out and sat him into a corner of the bed. She straightened Sherry's blanket and kissed her brow. It was smooth and a bit damp. Sherry didn't move.

Maren wandered back to her room and sighed. She couldn't go back to sleep; she was buoyed up as if she had drunk a gallon of coffee. With a frown, she opened her wardrobe. She might as well decide now what to wear tomorrow. She moved the hangers around. Really, she had nothing to wear. Nothing. With another sigh, she started to try on possible outfits.

In the end, she decided to wear a simple white linen dress with short sleeves and a light blue jacket. It was summery and professional without being too formal. The skirt flared out just above her knees, showing her shoes to advantage. Well, her left shoe, to be correct. She still had to wear a bandage around her right foot, which marred the optical impression somewhat. How could she be so nervous?

* * *

The door to Tony's restaurant stood wide open and allowed the fresh air and sun to float inside. Maren limped through the entrance and cleared her throat. Her hands felt damp.

"Hello?"

Nothing. The restaurant lay abandoned like a fairy-tale castle after showtime was over. Sunlight flooded through the tall windows and lit the burgundy cushions. The room smelled of wood and lemon detergent. Maren looked around. Nobody anywhere. "Hello?"

She heard a movement behind her and swiveled around. Tony's frame filled the door, silhouetted by the sunlight. As she squinted against the light, she couldn't make out his features, but she knew immediately that the man in front of her was Tony, not Chris. Why she knew it without a doubt, she had no clue. It scared her that she could discern the twins at one glance. It meant the difference she'd felt that night with Tony wasn't a product of her overactive imagination. She pulled herself together and went toward him with jelly-soft knees. Would he continue to pretend they didn't know each other? The question blocked the polite greeting she had prepared.

"Maren Christensen." His voice sounded like caramel. It wasn't a question, it was a statement, but the tone of his voice made it clear they were still on formal ground.

The disappointment made her limbs heavy. "Hi." Her greeting sounded like a croak, and she had to blink against the light.

He wore loose white trousers and a crisp blue linen

shirt that matched the color of his eyes. If he had been barefoot, he would have looked like the owner of a luxury yacht. Or rather like the advertisement for one. Maren suddenly felt dowdy in her dress. Before she could gather her wits to make some intelligent noises, Tony had propelled her outside to a small table at the side of the restaurant. An umbrella screened off the sun, and the weathered teak furniture looked inviting with the burgundy cushions on top. Maren smelled the resin of the firs trees again, the ones she had smelled when she had left the restaurant with him, still thinking he was Chris. The memory made her stomach curl.

"Take a seat. I'll be back in a moment," he said.

Maren sank onto the chair he had indicated. She placed her laptop on the table and set it up. The routine movements made her feel better. It was clear Tony had nothing but a business meeting in mind. She could relax. So why was she irritated? She leaned back, crossed her legs, and swung her left shoe to and fro.

He materialized at her shoulder, placed two long drinks onto the table, and sat across from her.

At her startled glance at the drink, he grinned and said, "No alcohol. Just orange juice, coconut milk, and vanilla ice cream."

Topped by a pineapple slice and a fancy cocktail stick that glitters with every move, Maren thought. *Quite a simple affair, really.* "I've never started a business meeting like that," she said, smiling, "but I could get used to it. Thank you."

His answering smile made her hurry on so she wouldn't forget her thoughts. "Now, what exactly did you have in mind? And how come you had the idea for a shared speech in the first place?"

He bent forward. "My brother told me about your business, and when the director of the Washington Culinary Institute called and asked if I wanted to tell the story of my restaurant, I thought it might be much more impressive if we presented a combined speech. Theory and practice together, so to speak."

"I see," Maren drew out the words. "And he went for it immediately?"

Tony smiled. "No. We still have to convince him. He said we should present the concept to him; that's why I asked to meet you."

"Hmm." Maren took a sip of her drink without taking her gaze off his face.

"You don't look enthusiastic," Tony said.

Maren suppressed a smile. His brother would have read her face too but instead of asking, he would have continued to battle her down with smooth talk. "I like the idea," she said. "In fact, it's great."

"I can tell. Your enthusiasm is foaming over."

She lifted her eyebrows. "What do you mean?"

"Ms. Christensen," he leaned back, "please . . ."

She couldn't bear it another minute and glared at him. "Please call me Maren."

He nodded. "Maren. Please tell me what you think, will you? It's obvious you're not enchanted."

Oh, but I am, Maren thought. *More than you will ever know.* She grabbed her glass and took a huge gulp. The tangy juice ran down her throat, followed by sweet vanilla. Finally, she put down her glass with a clank and said, "Okay. Barriers down." She took a breath. "What's in it for you?"

•

Chapter Seven

He blinked. "For me?"

"Yes, for you. Why bother with me at all? It would be less work to hold your speech without me, and be done with it."

His gaze dropped. Her laptop hummed in the silence. Maren balled her right fist. Was he going to lie again?

"When I started my restaurant," he finally said, "I made many mistakes. Some were trivial. Some almost broke my neck. If I tell the students my story, they will learn something. But if we bind it into a framework that can be applied to other situations as well, they'll profit much more."

Maren searched his face. His motives sounded too altruistic. Had he planned a trap somewhere? She had to be on her watch with the Mountforth twins.

A voice inside her said, "So what if he has ulterior motives? You gain in the bargain. Don't say no just because you fear something bad. If a hitch should appear, you can always back out." Sound thinking.

She took a deep breath and lifted her glass. "All right. Let's go for it."

His face broke into a smile that made her head dizzy. Their glasses tinkled as they touched, and for an instant, Maren forgot who she was and why she was here. It took all her self-control to remember her job.

Two hours later, they had set up a detailed structure in a PowerPoint presentation that covered everything from the initial dream to paying taxes on your first revenue.

Maren leaned back and sighed. "I don't want to sound vain, but I think we're onto something good here."

"It's not good, it's brilliant," he said. "And it's a pleasure to work with you."

She felt the blood rise up in her cheeks, but couldn't think of anything to say.

Tony smiled. "Don't you want to know why?"

She barely dared to meet his teasing eyes. "Well?"

"Because you know how to listen."

Maren lifted an eyebrow. "A perfect gift for a woman."

He shook his head. "I don't mean the kind of listening with tilted head, adoring gaze, and no brain. You listen intelligently. You ask questions, you shape everything into a structure, you find the holes in a concept."

She looked into her glass, a warm glow spreading

through her. "Thank you." She could have returned the compliment by saying that it was easy to criticize him, if that was a compliment? He didn't take anything personally. She couldn't help herself; she had to compare him to her ex-husband. Brad had been so focussed on his importance that every time she contradicted him, he was offended. It was relaxing to discuss a topic without having to take hurt feelings into account every cautious step of the way. But she kept the compliment to herself. She needed to keep her distance. If they worked well together, all the better. But that's where she drew the line.

She tried to ignore the feeling of loss as she left the restaurant. It had no reason to be there anyway.

"The Start-Up Company, Maren Christensen speaking."

"Maren? This is Tony."

Her heart beat faster. "Hi, Tony." Why had her voice sunk an octave? Did she want to sound sultry?

"I've just called Mr. Brown, the director of the Culinary Institute, and told him we're ready for our meeting."

"Great. What did he say?" Now she sounded like a squeaky pig.

"Unfortunately, he's on the brink of going to a seminar, so he can only see us in three weeks."

"Oh, no. Everything takes so long to happen. I hate that."

"You're impatient?"

She head the smile in his voice. They were getting onto dangerous ground. She had to stick to her rule, business only. "Yeah, well, who isn't?"

"I think we might use the time to work on our concept, to polish it," Tony suddenly said.

"Oh." Maren swallowed. He was right, of course. She couldn't draw back now. "Okay. At the restaurant?"

"Why not? What do you think about next Wednesday, at ten?"

Maren checked her book, still much too empty. "Fine." She stopped and took a breath. She should hang up now, but couldn't bring herself to do so. *Think, Maren! You've got to say something, something intelligent!* Her mind turned blank.

"Maren?" Tony's voice sounded soft.

Her heart missed a beat. "Yes?"

"It's nothing. Forget it."

She didn't dare to ask what he had wanted to say. "Good-bye." She felt small when she hung up, and all at once, tears burned in her eyes.

"It's too windy today to sit outside," Tony said, "but if we take table three, we'll have a good view."

"Sure. That's a good idea." Maren placed her laptop on the table he indicated. As she dropped into a chair, she tried not to think of her hair. On the short way from the car, the wind had blown it upside down, and now she probably looked like a crazy witch after a wild ride on her broom. She threw a sidelong glance at Tony. His hair was a bit ruffled, as usual, but she liked it that way. His light gray T-shirt seemed to have been molded over his chest and arms. Maren looked away. She had no time for sexy men. She had a job to do.

Her laptop took its time to hum to life. She looked out the window, toward the bay. Tony had built the car park behind the house so nothing marred the view in front. And as the restaurant was situated a bit higher than the terrace, the outside tables and chairs didn't obstruct the view either. Right behind them began a rocky stretch that dropped lower until it ended in a thin sickle of sand and reached the bay. The water glistened blue, with white foam caps crowning every small wave. They looked like dotted cream drops. Maren smiled. "If I worked here, you would fire me within a week."

He laughed. "Would I? Why?"

"Because I would stand around like a statue, lost in the beauty of your view instead of serving food."

He placed two strawberry smoothies on the table and took the chair on her right. Then he nodded toward the view. "It's my restaurant's best feature and my biggest handicap."

Maren looked at him in surprise. Major mistake . . . his blue-green eyes made her blood run too quick. "Handicap? Why?"

"I chose this restaurant because of the view." He sat

back and drew his hand through his hair. "No, that's not right. I fell for the view, then decided I would buy the restaurant here."

Maren frowned. "I don't see the difference."

"How many people live on Bainbridge Island?"

"More than twenty thousand, I believe. I've seen some statistics on the Internet recently, but they were a few years old."

"Okay. Take twenty thousand. That's not bad, but for a high-end restaurant, it's not a broad base, either. If I had followed my head and not my heart, I would have opened my restaurant over there." He made a move with his head toward the window.

Maren looked out. Across the bay, the skyline of Seattle stood like a ragged mountain. "Seattle, you mean?"

"Yes. Think of all the business companies with huge accounts, all the international guests who have to be taken for lunch. I can't complain; we're often booked out in the evenings, but lunch is a meager affair. There's not enough business on the island." He grinned. "Or rather, many people here are self-employed and they rarely treat themselves to a business lunch at Tony's."

"I see what you mean." Maren had never looked at the island from that point of view. Was it possible to drag more guests to the island some way or other? She took a sip of her strawberry smoothie. It tasted sweet and fresh, with a hint of lemon and coconut. The smooth liquid ran down her throat like cream. She'd never tasted anything as good. Boy, he knew how to mix a good drink, just as he knew how to cook. Occupied by her thoughts, she met his eyes and nodded.

One corner of his mouth lifted in a crooked smile.

She could get addicted to that smile. Maren quickly averted her gaze again. She had to be careful.

Tony made a move with his arm toward the bay. "Sometimes, I see the boats cruising by and wished I could haul them in for lunch with a huge harpoon."

Maren sat up straight and got a bit of strawberry down the wrong pipe. She choked and coughed.

Tony jumped up. "Are you all right?"

Maren waved her arm at him and tried to look as if she was in control, but her eyes streamed with tears and she gasped for breath. "Fi-hi-hine. I'm—hmmph—fine."

"Is it the cocktail? Are you allergic to strawberries?"

"No, oh, no." Maren shook her head and wiped her eyes. Darn. Her mascara was probably on its way toward her mouth by now, making her look like something the dog had spit out. Finally, she was able to take a deep breath. "The . . . the cocktail is fantastic. Thank you so much. I . . . I just had an idea, and that's why I—em—I swallowed something."

He smiled. "An idea?"

Maren waved her arm toward the bay. "Who owns the ground that stretches down to the water? Is it yours?"

"Yes."

"Why don't you build a jetty? You can deduct it from your gains if you declare it as a parking lot."

He stared at her. "A parking lot?"

"Yeah. You build it large enough for . . . say . . ." She frowned and rubbed her nose. "They always say you should think big, right?"

Tony lifted his eyebrows. "Yes?"

"Yes. Say six medium-size yachts."

He swallowed.

Maren beamed at him. The more she thought about it, the more she loved the idea. "You also need a sign . . . hmm." She jumped up. "Shall we have a look?"

He got up without taking his gaze from her. "By all means."

Maren rushed out of the restaurant, crossed the terrace with four long strides and started down the rocky stretch. The wind whipped up her hair with enthusiasm, and the air smelled of tang and salt. Maren took a deep breath.

Tony came up behind her. "Take my arm. At our last meeting, you still had a bandage on one ankle, didn't you? I don't want you to slip."

Maren closed her eyes for an instant. She didn't want to be close to him.

But he was right; she still had to be careful.

Be professional, she told herself. *Be cool.* Without looking at him, she grabbed his arm. "You would need to make some sort of path here." She pushed her hair out of her face and looked around. "It would still have to look natural, though, as if it had always been here. Maybe natural stone slabs, irregular, and small lights that lead the way. You don't want your guests to end up somewhere on the rocks."

He smiled at her. "Don't I?"

It was a mistake to look at him. He invited her to join in the joke, but his dark face was much too close, and if she leaned just a bit closer, she . . .

Maren dropped his arm and retreated a step. Behind her waves splashed against the shore. Maren whipped around and went to the very edge, until her feet stood on the white sickle of sand. "You need a sign to say it's a private parking lot for guests of the restaurant." She lifted her voice so he would hear her over the wind. "That would invite the people who happen to cruise by and have no clue that your restaurant exists. It should have your logo and at night, it should be illuminated."

Her hair kept flying into her mouth. She bunched it together with one hand, then swiveled around and looked back toward the restaurant. Its windows glistened in the sun. "Hmm. But on the other hand, you don't want to destroy the view from the restaurant. A garish neon light would ruin it all."

She heard his steps scrunch on the little pieces of rock just above the sand, then he said behind her, "We could build the jetty at the side."

Had he said *we*? Maren swallowed.

Tony pointed to the side. "My ground stretches quite a bit to the right."

Maren looked in the direction he indicated. A dark group of Douglas firs stood to their right, the wind roaring in their tops. "Over there, by the firs?" she said.

He laughed at her. "Yes. They're in the right position; they could screen the light."

As her eyes met his, the world receded. The wind dropped; the water stilled. Even the Douglas firs suddenly straightened, calm and serene. Maren's heart skipped a beat.

One corner of Tony's mouth lifted in that addictive smile. "Do you have any idea how great you look with windswept hair?"

It wouldn't do. She couldn't start to flirt, not now, not ever. She had no time for a man. Least of all, a man who had deceived her from the start. She swallowed. "Yep." She tried to make her voice as matter-of-fact as she could. "Like a woman with her fingers in a power socket." She turned and scrambled back toward the restaurant, uncomfortable because he would watch her. *I bet my skirt is crumpled at the back.*

As soon as they had regained the table, she opened her laptop and checked their presentation. "Can you believe it, we didn't put anything about location in here the last time," she said. "I think it should come right at the beginning."

"Yes, that's a good idea. Would you like another fruit smoothie?"

Maren didn't look up. "No, thanks."

She typed in a heading and a few sentences, then pushed the laptop over so he could see it. "What do you think about this?"

He bent forward. She liked the way his hair sprang back from his temple. It would be a pleasure to caress the hair at the nape of his neck and . . . Maren gave herself a shake. *Stop it!*

"It's great." Tony looked up. "During the presentation, we'll round it off with the story of the jetty. That was a brilliant idea, Maren. Thank you."

"It's okay." Maren averted her face. "In order to get the big shots over here, we could make a special mailing and send it to some CEOs." Had she said *we*? She hurried on, "It would be best if you could find out who owns a boat. Hmm . . . You would also have to put it into all the restaurant guides, as a special . . . and on your Web site . . . and . . ."

He held up his hands. "Hold on."

Maren could feel herself going red. "I'm sorry, I got swept away." She swallowed. "I didn't mean to . . ."

"That's not what I meant."

"No?"

"No. I wanted to ask if I could hire you for this project."

Maren took a deep breath. Had she heard him correctly? "Hire me?"

"Yes. I know it's not your core business, but would

you find the addresses of these CEOs, make leaflets, and get permission for the jetty, order it, organize the sign, the path, and so on? If you have the time, that is? I'm up to my eyebrows with my daily work because my chef got ill, and he's not quite recovered yet. I love the project, but I know I won't have the time for it."

Maren stared at him. It would mean money. Money she needed more than anything else. But it would also mean spending time with him. A lot of time. She wanted distance. She needed distance. But she also needed money. Darn. If only . . . if only they had met under different circumstances. "Em. Yes. Let me . . . let me think about it, and I'll send you a cost estimate. Okay?"

He smiled. "Sure."

It took Maren three solid hours to make a project plan and a cost estimate. At first, she wondered if she should make it so expensive that he could only say no. But no, that was unprofessional. She wasn't in a position to fling orders away. So she finished it off as best as she could and mailed it to him.

His reply came the same day. She had the job.

Maren swallowed. Was there a word that combined *darn* and *hurray*?

The preparations for the Swedish summer night filled all Tony's free time. He wanted to impress Maren's father, but most of all, he wanted to impress Maren. In spite of the jetty project and their meetings, Maren had kept her distance, had never allowed him a glimpse of her personal life. Whenever he did some careful probing, she blocked him with polite but firm smiles and elegant changes of topic. Every compliment was turned down, every smile froze as soon as he tried to get closer. And he had never seen her laugh. It infuriated him, and yet, he understood. He wished he could explain the situation to her. He wished he could tell her why he'd taken his brother's place that night but every time he thought he couldn't stand it anymore, Chris' voice rang in his ears: ". . . and if you breathe a word to Maren . . ."

He couldn't do it. So he contented himself with discussing their presentation, and whenever she wasn't around, he concentrated on making the Swedish summer night so perfect, it would convince even the most hard-boiled Swede. He paid Belinda for sewing long pinafores in dark blue with the distinctive yellow cross of the Swedish flag, and prepared blue-and-yellow signs explaining the dishes. It was easy to buy small Swedish flags to top up the dishes and bright yellow paper napkins; a lot harder to find an inexpensive copy shop that mounted two huge pictures onto thin wooden boards. He had chosen summery pictures of the typical Swedish red-and-white houses surrounded by poppy plants and blue corn flowers. He planned to use them as dividers between the buffet and the house wall, leaving the room in between to store supplies he needed close at hand.

When the Swedish summer evening came, his crew was ready. He split them up and left the restaurant in the care of Guiseppe, who was by now back in form. Thank God for Guiseppe.

Now, with every dish in place, Tony stood behind the buffet. His stomach churned at the thought that he might have forgotten something, but even more because he would see Maren soon.

He scanned the garden looking for her and noticed a small girl standing at the side. Two huge yellow bows made her pigtails stand away from her head like horizontal brushes. White and yellow flowers on her dress matched the bows.

"Hi, there," Tony said. "Want a meatball?"

She shook her head and continued to stare at the table.

"A bit of cake, maybe?"

She turned her blue eyes to him. "Do you have melon?" Her tone suggested she had asked for a Barbie Castle complete with wedding guests.

"Hmm, let me see." Tony smothered a smile, went to the left side of the buffet, and selected a dish. "Yes, I do."

The little girl inspected the bowl. "That's not melon," she said.

"I assure you, it is."

"No, it's not. A melon is big and cut into slices. Big, big slices." She indicated a slice the size of a dachshund. These."—she pointed at the dish—"are little round balls!" Her gaze reproached him.

He found her irresistible. "Yes, because I cut them that way. See . . ." Tony rummaged in his supply box behind the divider and retrieved the scoop spoon. "With this special spoon, I can cut little balls out of the melon."

"Wow." She stared at the spoon. "Then you never ruin your dress when you eat a melon?"

"Never." If the other guests were like her, it was going to be a great night.

"Can I have the whole bowl?"

"The whole bowl?" Tony stared at her.

She giggled. A delightful, carefree giggle. A giggle he could get addicted to.

Had he seen her before? Her face reminded him of someone.

"Yes. Mommy says they're my vice. I can eat a whole melon for dinner, you know." Her small fingers plucked a melon ball and dropped it into her mouth. "Do you have a vice too?"

He laughed. "You bet. Plenty of them."

"Really? Mommy says one or two are enough. What's your vice?" Another ball vanished.

Tony suppressed the temptation to capture one of the bouncing pigtails. Instead, he watched her hover over the bowl and select another melon ball. "Hmm. I have a passion for marshmallows."

"Marshmallows?" She swallowed. "Yes, they're nice. I like them too. Mommy hates them. She has a vice too, and you'll never guess what it is."

He couldn't help it, he had to laugh. "Maybe you shouldn't tell me, then."

The little girl shrugged. "Oh, she wouldn't mind. You see, she's a bit weird sometimes, but in general, she's nice. She eats white gummy bears."

He blinked. "She eats what?"

"White gummy bears. She also takes the red, but she hates the other colors." She crowed with laughter. "See, I told you it's funny."

Tony grinned. "Does she eat them often?"

The pigtails wobbled. "No, no. She only chews them when she's worried. She says it's sooooothing."

"I see." Tony watched as the melon balls vanished at an alarming rate. "And your dad, does he have a vice too?"

The girl shrugged. "I don't know, I don't see him much." Two more melon balls disappeared.

He grinned down at her. "Would you tell me your name?"

"Sherry."

"Nice to meet you, Sherry. I'm Tony."

She grinned at him, her mouth smeared with bits of melon. "My Mommy knows a Tony too. She says he's handsome and—"

"Sherry! Here you are! I've looked for you every-where. We have to—"

Tony and Sherry whirled around. Maren stood in front of them.

Now he knew why Sherry looked familiar. Mother and daughter had the same wide mouth, same small nose. His mouth went dry.

Chapter Eight

Maren gasped. "Tony! What are you doing here?" Her dress matched her daughter's in design, held by two thin straps over smooth brown shoulders.

Tony dragged his gaze away and pointed toward the buffet. He tried to speak, but nothing came out. With an effort, he cleared his throat. "I'm doing the catering for the night."

She stared from the buffet to him, to her daughter. "But I . . . I thought you . . . I . . ."

Her father appeared behind her. "Tony! I must say the buffet looks marvelous. It's exactly what I wanted."

Maren stared at him. "But you . . . you never told me Tony was doing the catering."

Lars shook his head. "Didn't I? I thought you knew.

111

He saved us. Gorny's Catering went bankrupt two weeks ago, haven't you heard?"

Sherry darted to her mother. "Mommy, you can shape melon into balls! Can I have a spoon like that? And Mommy, his vice is a passion for marshmallows, and he's my friend, and his name is Tony too, just like the man you—"

"One moment, Sherry." Maren caught her daughter by the shoulders and held her away. "I told you not to eat melon until you've given your surprise to Granddad."

Tony grabbed a yellow napkin and handed it to Sherry, who wiped her mouth with so much vigor, bits of melon squash ended up on her cheekbones. "But listen!" Sherry hopped up and down. "They're not slices, they're balls, and purrfectly safe to eat, because, look, they're small, and you can drop them into your mouth, like this . . . see?" Another melon dropped with an audible plop into Sherry's mouth.

Sherry's grandfather chortled, and Tony couldn't suppress a grin.

Maren looked up and met Tony's eyes.

He could see the struggle going on inside her, but finally, she broke into laughter.

Tony grabbed the edge of the buffet table to steady himself.

"Lars, Maren, come here!" A voice called from within the house. "The first guests have just turned into the drive!"

*　　*　　*

The next two hours Tony and his team drowned in a whirl of work, offering dishes, replenishing the buffet, answering questions. Tony served Annie and made sure he pretended not to know her, but he felt uncomfortable as she searched his face without trying to hide it. He had the feeling she saw more than necessary. He was glad Chris was nowhere in the vicinity.

But no matter how busy he was, Tony was always aware of Maren's presence. Whenever she came close to the buffet, a tingle ran down his spine. He tried to probe into his feelings upon discovering that she had a daughter, and was astonished to find that it fascinated him. If Sherry didn't look like a miniature of Maren, it might have been different, but as it was, he soon started to look for her little face bobbing in and out of the throng.

As for Sherry, she was convinced they were the best of friends and came in regular intervals to stock up on melon balls. He was just replenishing her little bowl when a surprised voice said, "Anthony!"

Tony knew that voice. He pressed the bowl into Sherry's dirty hands, straightened, and slowly turned around. "Hi, Dad."

His father stared at him, a plate forgotten in his hand. "What are you doing here? I thought you're always needed at that restaurant of yours."

"I'm responsible for the catering tonight." Tony wished his father would for once look pleased.

"But . . . a caterer? My son?"

"I offered it as an emergency help. Lars Christensen's caterer went bankrupt two weeks ago."

His father passed a hand over his brow. "Yes, yes, I see. I hope you won't do it more often, though."

Tony clenched his teeth. "And how come you're here tonight? I wasn't aware you knew Lars." The minute the words were out of his mouth, he heard Chris' voice again. "Maren's father is one of Dad's golf buddies." Darn. If he had remembered, he would have thought twice about accepting the job.

His father looked at Tony over his glasses. How Tony hated that superior look. "But Lars and I have played in a foursome together for years. Surely you knew that?"

Tony sighed. How little he knew about his father. Ever since his choice of career, he kept a safe distance from his parents because their disapproval hurt. "Hmm. I know Maren Christensen is a customer of yours, isn't she?"

His father nodded and looked over the buffet, then selected one piece of crisp bread with smoked salmon as if he was offered a selection of worms.

Tony clenched his hands. *Steady, old boy.* "Chris told me he's handling her account."

That earned him another glance over the top of the glasses. "Really? And since when are you interested in our office affairs?"

Tony felt hot fury shooting up inside him. He forced a laugh. "Oh, I still think it's dusty and boring, don't you worry. I'm just trying some small talk to keep up appearances."

He turned to a lady with pink hair who just arrived at the buffet and smiled at her. "Can I help you with your selection, ma'am?"

When the sun set, Maren's mother distributed tiny hurricane lights all over the garden. As the evening got late, things turned quieter at the buffet. Tony sent his staff home, filled a huge glass with lemon water, and withdrew to the shadow next to his dividers. He dropped onto an upturned bucket, leaned his back against the house wall, and took a deep breath. The meeting with his father still rankled him. He shouldn't have lost it. Wasn't it stupid how much it mattered that his parents appreciated him? By rights, he should have stopped caring long ago. Instead, he felt like hired help whenever his parents were around. Tony sighed.

He hadn't seen Maren for an hour. Maybe she was somewhere in the back of the garden, dancing with some lucky guy. But her laugh earlier in the evening had been worth it. They had never laughed together. He relived the moment. It had been all he hoped for—and more. Her mouth bewitched him. He shook his head and took a gulp of lemon water.

A little voice next to him whispered, "We could build a fort behind the posters with the Swedish houses." Sherry.

He grinned in spite of himself and whispered back, "I'd rather not. They topple over too easily. I'm sure your mother has prepared a cozy bed for you somewhere."

"Phew," Sherry shook her head so hard, her now-crooked pigtails flew into all directions. She dropped onto the floor next to him and drew up her knees beneath her skirt, revealing several stains on her crumpled dress. "I'm not going to bed tonight. Mommy said I can stay awake as long as I want."

"Aren't you lucky."

They were quiet for a moment. Tony's legs ached. If only someone told him he could sleep as long as he wanted. Something touched his arm, and he felt Sherry's head leaning against his side. A feeling gripped him, a feeling he had never known before . . . tenderness, mixed with a longing to protect and something else, indescribable, sweet.

"Tony," Sherry said, "do you want to dance with me?"

"I'd love to, my fair lady"—Tony tugged a little at one crooked pigtail—"but I'm on duty tonight, so I'm not supposed to dance."

"What does 'on duty' mean?"

"It means I'm not a guest. I work here."

"Oh." Sherry digested this. "I wished Mr. Poppy was on duty too."

"Mr. Poppy?"

"He already danced three times with Mommy."

Tony sat up straight. "Oh?"

"I don't like him." Sherry shrugged. "His name isn't Poppy, but I call him like that. You know why?"

"Why?"

"He looks like Poppy. Do you know Poppy?"

"No." Tony swallowed.

"Poppy is Carol's dog. Carol is my dearest friend. And Poppy is a sweet dog, a . . . a . . . I forget what it's called, but he has a punched-in nose." She pressed her fist against her nose. "As if he ran against the wall."

In spite of his stormy feelings, Tony had to smother a smile. "But maybe Mr. Poppy is kind?"

Sherry shook her head. "Nah. He told me a girl shouldn't run and shouldn't sit in the grass. That's stupid, isn't it?"

"Very."

"He told me I should take better care of my dress, shouldn't climb and shouldn't play turtle. He even said I shouldn't eat melons! Can you imagine?"

"I can see there's just one solution." Tony lowered his voice and rolled his eyes. "We have to throw him out of the garden."

Sherry giggled and pointed toward the back of the garden, where a few couples danced. "He's over there, with Mom."

Tony wished he could punch Mr. Poppy's nose into an even flatter shape.

"Ssh! Here they come!"

They watched from their retreat in the shadow as Maren and her dance partner came toward the buffet. His elegant jacket brushed Maren's arm in a way that made Tony hiss under his breath. At least the guy didn't put his arm around her shoulders. Maren looked around, and Tony hoped she was wondering where he was, but then he heard her say, "I haven't seen Sherry for ages."

"Oh, she'll be around somewhere." The light from the living room fell onto the man's face. Sherry was right, the resemblance to a bull terrier was uncanny.

He stepped closer. "Maren . . ."

"Hmm? Have you seen if there's some of that sponge cake left?"

He barely glanced at the buffet. "No, I think it's all gone."

Tony frowned.

Mr. Poppy took a deep breath. "Maren, when I came to the party tonight, I had no idea what a wonderful woman I would meet. I think you know how I feel about you. I'd like to ask you if . . ."

Tony felt Sherry's slight form next to him trembling with suppressed emotion. Or was it his own body? Her small hand clamped on top of his arm. It hurt, but he didn't care.

Mr. Poppy-Nose continued, ". . . we couldn't have dinner somewhere next week?"

At that instant, Sherry jumped forward, ducked beneath the table, shot out on the other side, and threw herself into her mother's arms. "Mommy!"

Tony smiled. Little vixen.

An hour later, he found Sherry half-hidden by his divider. With the help of some cushions from the sofa in the living room and a blanket she had fashioned herself a small nest in the shadow of the house. Now she was fast asleep. As he looked at her round cheeks and crooked pigtails, he suddenly felt it again, that strange wave of tenderness. He couldn't turn away. How precious she was. It seemed strange to see her so quiet.

She moved in her sleep and mumbled something. He bent down and drew the blanket a bit higher. How much like Maren she looked. He swallowed, forced himself to turn his back on her and left the buffet to find Maren. If only she wasn't with Mr. Poppy-Nose.

He discovered her standing next to a towering bush with fragrant flowers he didn't know. They smelled of vanilla and looked large and white in the moonlight. Maren stood with her back half-turned to him and talked to a man he couldn't make out in the shadow of the bush. Then the man spoke.

Tony closed his eyes. It was his father.

"My son told me you've stopped working with us, Ms. Christensen."

Tony stiffened. Had he heard him correctly? Maren had dropped them? Darn. They could have had that without changing roles.

His father's voice rustled like a dry leaf. "If it has anything to do with the financial side of it, we would be more than ready to waive the fees for some time, you know. Your father told me that . . . it might be a problem."

Maren's shoulders looked tense. She bowed her head and stared into her glass.

Tony didn't dare to move.

Finally, Maren said with a low voice, "Thank you, Mr. Mountforth, that's very kind. I do appreciate the offer, but I'm afraid I can't accept it."

Magnus Mountforth cleared his throat. "You know, you're the daughter of an old friend. Your father and I have helped each other a lot over the years, and it's only natural that—"

"No." Maren's voice was clear. "As I said, I'm grateful—more than grateful—for your kind offer; I know it's something special, but . . ." Tony could hear her swallow." . . . but I'm afraid I can't do that."

Tony knew his father would insist even before he heard him speak. "You know, it's not good to have too much pride, girl."

Maren took a deep breath. Her shoulders turned stiffer by the minute. "I . . . I know. I assure you, it's not misplaced pride."

Tony felt a stab of admiration. She could have listed all the reasons she had given him on the boat. It would be enough to convince his father of Chris' uselessness. Instead, she kept on neutral ground. What had Chris said about her? *No matter how angry she is, she will always remain in control.*

But Maren didn't know his father. It was obvious he had put it into his head to keep Maren as a customer, and he wouldn't accept no for an answer. She would be forced to give a reason soon.

Tony hesitated. Maybe he should interrupt them.

Then again, no. Whenever he said anything against Chris, his father thought it was jealousy. If Maren did, maybe it would sink in. And maybe it would make his father act, and Chris would find something new, something that made him happy in the long run, even if it was painful now. He bit his lips in indecision.

His father said, "You see, I not only promised your father to help you, I also believe you're an admirable young woman with a shrewd head on your shoulders. I'd like to keep you as our customer."

Maren drew herself up. "Mr. Mountforth, I can't tell you how much I appreciate your compliment and your offer, but I honestly can't accept it. I . . . I have found another tax consultant in the meantime."

Ouch. Tony flinched.

The leaves in the bush rustled with the breeze and from the end of the garden, they heard laughter. Magnus Mountforth cleared his throat. "Is it because of my son? He asked me to transfer your account to someone else." His voice sounded pained.

So Chris had done that? Tony felt a bit better.

"Your . . . your son and I . . ." Maren seemed to hunt for words." . . . we . . . we didn't exactly see eye to eye, that's true."

"I see."

The note of defeat in his father's voice pierced Tony, and he couldn't bear it anymore.

"Maren."

She swiveled around.

"Sherry fell asleep behind the buffet. She's warm and safe, so I believe you can leave her there, but I wanted to tell you, so you wouldn't look for her."

The moonlight showed her feelings flitting across her face, gone in seconds. Anger because Chris had put her into a situation where she appeared foolish in front of his father, concern for Sherry, gratefulness to be told where she was.

The urge to tell her everything choked him, but he couldn't, just as she couldn't tell his father about Chris. Who had invented moral codes anyway? He would tackle Chris again. Tomorrow.

"I'll be in touch." His father nodded at Maren and turned toward the house. Tony followed him with his gaze as he went up the lawn. His shoulders sagged a little, and for the first time, he looked old. Without thinking, he said the first words that came to his head. "If he didn't plan our lives, he wouldn't be so disappointed when we don't comply."

Maren was surprised. A minute ago, it had taken all her self-control not to glower at them, not to say to Magnus Mountforth, "Why don't you ask your precious sons why I dropped your account?" She had already half-turned away when she caught the look of regret on Tony's face and heard his words. They made her stop in her tracks and defend Magnus. "Every parent makes plans."

He looked at her. "You may make plans for Sherry,

but you wouldn't ridicule her if she chose another track, would you?"

Maren swallowed. "I hope not."

He didn't have to say his father had done just that.

Maren shook herself. "Anyway, your brother is a grown man and can decide for himself what he wants."

"My father has a strong personality."

"Sure." Maren nodded. "But if Chris wanted to, he could overcome him. After all, you managed it, didn't you?"

He lifted his eyebrows. "So there's no difference between us?" His voice sounded casual.

Maren caught her breath and retreated a step. *There's all the difference in the world. Your brother hasn't even once made my heart beat faster.* She forced a laugh. "Well, what do you want? You're twins after all."

"Yes." His voice was flat. "We are."

Maren frowned. They had continued their discussion on the boat. Had he noticed? Why, oh why didn't he tell her about the deception? Why did he pretend it had never happened? If only she could trust him. But she had trusted once already, and it had been foolish. *If a man starts with a lie, it can only go downhill,* her inner voice said. Maren tried to collect her wits and turned toward the house. "Thank you for telling me about Sherry. I already looked for her before I fell into the conversation with your father."

He fell into step beside her. "She's enchanting."

Maren had to smile. "She demolished your complete melon stock within one hour, didn't she? I hope she didn't get on your nerves."

"On the contrary. She's sweet and natural."

"Thank you. She's a bit wild at times."

He stopped. The expression in his eyes made her knees wobble. "You know, she reminds me of her mother."

Maren's heart started to race. "Me? I . . . I'm not wild."

He laughed. "Aren't you? To me, you seem like a well-controlled tiger."

Chapter Nine

Hot irons hammered against her forehead from the inside out. She would have to take another ibuprofen soon. But not yet. She would not get up from her desk before her account was done. She would not think about Tony, about the things he had said, about the feelings he had started inside her; feelings that should have been dead and buried long ago.

Maren pushed back her hair with a sigh and continued to enter her figures. Her hand trembled a little when she finally hit Enter on her keyboard and looked at the last sum of her June balance sheet: −$235.93.

She grabbed a white gummy bear, pushed it into her mouth, and chewed with a frown. Six months. She only had six more months in order to turn it into a profit—a profit that would allow her and Sherry to make a living.

She stared at the figures. True, there was an upward curve. May had finished with a bigger loss. And she had Tony's jetty project. It was a nice sum, bigger than any she had ever earned. On the other hand, could she count it? Would he have given her that project if . . . if he wasn't attracted to her? Besides, she didn't know if he would pay. Maybe, if she didn't agree to go out with him, he would take his revenge by ignoring her bill. Maren shuddered. No, better not count it. Not until she had the money on her account.

Maren calculated once again. If her figures improved in the same mini steps each month, she would end up with −$3.62 by the time she had used up her investment budget.

Her head ached even more, and she wished she could lie down on her bed, with a cool cloth over her eyes. She wished she could curl up and cry.

She had to think up something. There were thousands of people out there who started up their businesses. She just had to find them.

Maybe the speech at the Culinary Institute would help. If Mr. Brown accepted her. Oh, how she hoped he would.

Henry Barker Productions still had not answered her query. Should she call them? But no, their Web site had been explicit. If you call them, you lose all chances of getting onto *Noteworthy Enterprises.* She sighed again.

Mr. Brown was a much better bet. She should be grateful to Tony. Maren rubbed her temples. No, better not think about Tony. She had to think about her business. Maybe she could contact a few business schools and offer to make similar speeches, against a fee, of course. Yes, that was a good idea. She would have to hunt up addresses on the Internet. She couldn't take schools that were too far away, otherwise she would have to leave Sherry too long. Sherry liked to stay with her grandparents, but Maren hated to ask them. They had done enough for her. It was time she stood on her own feet.

If only her head didn't hurt so much. If only Tony's face didn't distract her by appearing on the screen whenever she didn't focus enough. She didn't need a man in her life. Sherry's father, Brad, had caused enough complications, and it had taken much too long to shake herself free of him. She had more than enough on her plate. A man needed time and energy. She had neither. She had Sherry. And although Sherry sometimes asked for a father, she seemed happy enough. She wasn't used to a man in the house, to another presence claiming her mother.

Maren started to shake herself, but immediately stopped. It felt as if red-hot metal rods clashed together in her head.

At that moment, Sherry tumbled from the garden through the door. She cried, but not the "I've fallen and need a hug" cry, not the "I'm upset because I dropped my sweets into the dirt" cry, but a high, piercing cry, a cry that spoke of agony and fear. Maren shot up. "Sherry! What happened?"

Sherry gulped for air, her face wet with tears. "A . . . a spli . . . a spli . . . a splinter, Mommy."

Maren grabbed Sherry and pressed her against her chest. "Shh, calm down. Calm down, darling. Show me the splinter."

"It's here, here!" Sherry wriggled out of her arms and held up her foot.

Maren clenched her teeth. Blood made her queasy, and whenever Sherry was hurt, she had to fight the urge to run away while praying for a miracle. She saw the splinters immediately. Two, one deep and large, the other small and thin. Maren gulped and said, "All right, darling. I'll take it out." She gathered Sherry into her arms and sat her on the sofa. "I'll be back in a second."

Maren ran to Sherry's room; the pain in her head increasing with every jerk. She collected Pimm, rushed into the bathroom, got tweezers, a needle, some iodine, and shot down the stairs again, all the time trying to move like a hovercraft to avoid more pain in her head.

"Here's Pimm." She pressed the teddy bear into Sherry's arms. "Hold him tight. Now give me your foot, and don't move."

Sherry grabbed Pimm and pulled up her legs to her chest, so Maren couldn't get at them. Her eyes widened until the white showed all around the iris. "It'll hurt!" Her voice pierced Maren's ear. "I know it will."

Maren swallowed. She knew Sherry could work herself into hysteria within two seconds. The last time, it had been a broken fingernail and before that, a cough syrup Sherry had hated.

"Sherry." Maren tried to ignore her throbbing head, tried to make her voice calm and patient. "You know I have to get it out. I'll be as quick as possible, but you have to stop twisting and moving, otherwise it'll hurt much more. Okay?" She took Sherry's foot and tried to pull it toward her.

"No, no, noooo." Sherry threw herself against the cushions and kicked and squirmed until Maren released the foot.

She gathered Sherry into her arms. "Shhh, no panic. Now take a deep breath . . . There. You are a big girl, and you have to be strong. If you make a huge effort and control yourself, I . . . I'll let you sleep in my bed tonight, okay?"

Sherry hiccuped and nodded. Maren closed her eyes for a moment. It felt as if her lids were on fire. She sat Sherry down again and knelt in front of her. If only she didn't feel so queasy. Her hand trembled as she grabbed the tweezers and tackled the big splinter.

There! She got hold of it and pulled. It slid out without a hitch. Phew. Maren beamed. "I've got the large one. Look here," she held up the tweezers with the splinter, "it was huge. And you were brave like a lion, love. It didn't hurt, did it?"

Sherry threw her a look full of scorn and withdrew her foot. "It hurt awfffully."

"Give me your foot," Maren said and caught Sherry's

leg, "I still have to get the small splinter." Maren pulled her lower lip between her teeth and tried to grab the small splinter with the tweezers, but it had slid horizontally below the skin. Darn. She put away the tweezers and reached for the needle to prick up the skin.

Sherry jumped. "No, nooo, Mommy! Not the needle! You'll hurt me with the needle!"

"Keep still!" Maren held onto the squirming foot. "It will only hurt if you jump around. I'm just going to lift up the skin a bit. It won't hurt, really!"

Sherry kicked her leg up and down until Maren had to let go. "No, noo, it'll hurt, I know it will!"

Maren sat back on her haunches and glared at Sherry. "Do you want to go to the hospital with me?"

"Nooo!"

"Then will you please stay quiet now?" Maren made sure her voice sounded serious.

"Noo, I'm afraid, Mommy. I'm so afraid."

Maren stared at her daughter's tear-streaked face. If only she knew how much of Sherry's fit was fear and how much was a full-blown theater performance. "You only have to be afraid if you move. If you keep still just a minute, I can take it out. All right?"

But Sherry was past it. She squirmed and thrashed on the sofa so Maren couldn't hold her down. Finally, she let go. "Sherry, if you don't keep still now, you won't get any dessert tonight."

It didn't help. Sherry continued crying, and whenever Maren tried to take her foot, she pulled it away.

Maren tried logic, she tried persuasion, she tried threats, she tried force, but it was all in vain. Sherry shouted and cried as if Maren tortured her in the most sadistic way possible. Maren clenched her teeth. In a minute, the neighbors would believe she was abusing her daughter and call the police. She wiped her forehead and suppressed the urge to shake Sherry. Her head felt as if it would explode into a million screaming bits any second. Then a flying kick from Sherry hit her on the shin.

Maren threw the needle and tweezers on the table, dripped a bit of iodine in the general direction of Sherry's foot and jumped up. "All right, Sherry!" Her voice reverberated through the room and made the windows rattle. "I'll leave the splinter in, since you refuse to behave."

Sherry threw up both her arms and wailed, "Noo, nooo, Mommy." She hiccuped. "If you leave the splinter in, it'll infect itself, and my foot will turn black, and then it'll fall off, and then I'll . . ." Her voice rose to a scream, "I'll die!"

Maren blinked, stunned by Sherry's scenario.

"I don't want to die! I'm too young to die!"

Maren broke into tears and laughter at the same time. She hid her face in her hands and collapsed onto the sofa next to Sherry. She laughed and cried until she couldn't see anything anymore.

"Mommy?" Sherry's hand stole into hers. "Are you all right?"

Maren sniffed. She found a tissue in her pocket and blew her nose. "I'm okay. Don't worry." She took a deep breath and pulled herself together. She had to try one more time. Maybe her outburst had shocked Sherry into obedience. "Sweetheart, you won't die if you let me take the splinter." She bent down to take Sherry's leg. With the move, her headache grew more intense.

Sherry started to kick again. "No! Not the needle!"

Maren took a deep breath. Should she take Sherry to the hospital? Better not. Sherry would manage to create an even bigger uproar with more audience around. Besides, they couldn't give her a general anesthesia just for one tiny splinter. Maren gave up.

So the splinter remained, and Maren prayed it would not get infected.

Later that night, when she lay in bed, she wondered if a man would have been able to calm Sherry down. She sighed. Maybe. Maybe not. But it wasn't an option. She had to cope on her own.

"Chris, this is Tony. Why don't you pick up your phone when I call? I need to talk to you."

Tony slammed down the receiver with a suppressed oath. He knew Chris didn't call him back because he didn't want to allow him to tell Maren the truth.

Tony sighed. How he hated to pretend he had never taken Chris' place. He picked up the receiver with a frown and dialed Maren's number.

The phone rang once, then he heard Sherry's voice. "Hello?"

"Hi Sherry, this is Tony."

"Tony!" Sherry's high voice squeaked into his ear. "I'm going to be in a school dance. I will be Annabel and Carol will be Annalisa. We're flowers."

Tony had no clue what she was talking about, but he didn't have the heart to admit it. "That sounds great." Just in time, he thought about a question that might fit. "Will you get special costumes?"

"Yes, mine will be pink and green, and Carol's is rose and green. She has big flowers on hers, and I have small flowers." Her voice lost its exuberance. "I like her flowers better, but . . ." Her voice went up again, ". . . pink is prettier than rose, don't you think?"

"Absolutely." Tony grinned. "I bet your mom is proud of you. Is she around?"

"Yes, but she doesn't have time right now."

Tony tried not to feel snubbed, but he couldn't overcome the feeling. Did he do something wrong at her father's birthday? They hadn't talked since that night.

Sherry said, "Mommy is in the bathroom and painting her toenails. She stuck little pieces of . . . of something between her toes, so she can't walk, only hop, and the last time she did that, she fell down and had a—"

"Sherry!" Maren's voice came from the background. "Who are you talking to?"

"It's Tony, Mommy."

Absolute silence reverberated though the receiver. Tony grinned. The receiver clanked and Maren's voice, almost as smooth and professional as usual, came down the line, "Hello, Tony. What can I do for you?"

He could imagine how she felt, but the picture Sherry had painted still lingered in his mind. He cleared his throat. "You have a charming secretary."

"Yes." Her voice sounded rueful. "A bit indiscreet at times, but otherwise, perfect."

"I called to let you know that Mr. Brown asked to see us next Tuesday at ten. Would that be okay for you?"

He heard paper rustling through the receiver. Then she said, "Yes, fine."

"I'll come to pick you up, if that's okay?"

"No, let's do it the other way round. I'll pick you up at the restaurant."

"Okay." When Tony hung up, he suppressed a sigh. With practiced skill, she kept him at a safe distance. If only he knew how to get behind her barrier. If only Chris would allow him to come clean. If only he had met her under different circumstances. Maybe the meeting at the Culinary Institute would allow him to get closer. Maybe.

"Mommy, how many times do I need to sleep until the day of the dance?" Sherry lay beneath her Barbie spread, Pimm tucked into the crook of her arm.

"Twelve more nights, darling."

Sherry sighed and rolled her eyes. "That's soou long."

Maren ruffled her hair. "But it gives you more time to practice."

"You'll come and watch me from the au-di-ence, won't you, Mommy?"

Maren smiled at the careful way Sherry pronounced the word. "Yes, I'll come."

"And you'll clap your hands when we're done?"

"Yes, of course."

"And you'll get up and shout *anchor*, won't you?"

Maren laughed. "I might even do that."

"Why do people shout *anchor*, Mommy?"

"It's not anchor, it's *encore*. That's French, and it means 'again' or in this case, 'more,' Sherry."

Her daughter wrinkled her nose and thought about it. Finally, she said, "Mommy?"

"Yes?"

"Kerry's mother can't come, and Kerry is sad. But you will come, won't you, Mommy?"

"Yes, my dear. Now stop worrying about it, and go to sleep."

"And you'll come?" Sherry looked at her with an anxious gaze.

"Yes. I promise. Come hell or high water, I will come."

"Hell? Why hell?"

Maren didn't know if she should laugh or sigh. "Oh, darling, it's a proverb. It means whatever happens, I'll come, and I'll clap, and I'll shout anchor. So stop worrying, and let me have a look at your foot."

"Why?" Sherry frowned but she obeyed, and pushed her foot out from beneath the blanket.

"Because I need to check on your famous splinter. If it's bad, you can't dance." She examined the little pink sole of her daughter's foot and drew a sigh of relief.

"It's fine. The splinter seems to have found its own way out."

Her eyes met Sherry's and held them for a while. They had been lucky. Maren tried not to wonder about the future, about the scenes she would have to live through if Sherry ever had another splinter or had to take a medicine she despised. She wondered again if Sherry would have obeyed a father, then shrugged and bent to give her a kiss. "Good night, darling."

"The Start-Up Company, Maren Christensen speaking."

"Ms. Christensen? Henry Barker Productions. This is Dolly Plow."

Maren sat up straight. Her heart did a somersault. Henry Barker Productions? Were they interested in her company profile for *Noteworthy Enterprises*? She tried to make her voice sound firm and professional. "Good morning, Ms. Plow. How can I help you?"

"Mr. Barker liked your query and would like to see you. Will the twenty-third at four o'clock be all right?"

Maren ruffled through the pages of her diary with a trembling hand. The twenty-third. Somehow that date rang a bell. Didn't she have an appointment that day? The dentist? Whatever it was, she would cancel it. She got to the right page.

Oh, no. Maren's heart sank. Sherry's dance at school started at six o'clock . . . the twenty-third. No way could she return from Seattle in time if she had the interview with Henry Barker at four. She cleared her throat. "The twenty-third is a bit tight." Her voice sounded rough. "Would another date be possible? How about the twenty-second?"

"I'm sorry." The secretary sounded affronted, as if Maren had asked the moon to change its course. "It's either the twenty-third or nothing."

Maren clenched her teeth, her brain in a panic. She had to find a way. She had to! "I see. Er . . . would it be possible to schedule a date in the morning? I could manage that."

"Mr. Barker has a meeting all morning." The secretary didn't add "and you are getting on my nerves," but her tone implied it.

"Right." Maren swallowed. She had to find a solution. Now! "How long would the meeting approximately last?"

"Oh, half an hour, sometimes more, sometimes less."

Now Dolly sounded bored and Maren could almost see her inspecting her bloodred fingernails with a sour mouth. Maren did a quick calculation. "Well, in that case, I could come at three o'clock." Even if the meeting took one hour, she could leave by four, catch the ferry at four forty and arrive in time for Sherry's dance with time to spare. For good measure, she added, "I do appreciate your flexibility," and held her breath.

There was a slight popping sound. Could it be the secretary had just blown a bubble of chewing gum? Maren felt like scratching the inside of her ear.

"Weeeell." Dolly drew out the word. It did sound

bubble-gummy. "I could try to slip you into that slot. But mind you, it's not convenient."

Maren wanted to hit her. "All the more thanks for managing it." She hoped Dolly would not catch the note of irony in her voice.

"At three, then. Good-bye, Ms. Christensen."

"Good-bye." Maren threw down the receiver. What an awful woman!

But what a great opportunity! Her chin in her hands, she drifted into a daydream. If Henry Barker Productions took her on, it would mean so much. People would call her from all over the state. She might be asked to give interviews or readings, and clients would come in . . .

Sherry skipped through the door. "Mommy, can I invite a friend to the dance?"

Maren needed a minute to return from her dream and focus on her daughter. "But you've already invited everybody, Sherry! Grandma and Granddad promised to come." She didn't mention Sherry's father, who had claimed to be busy, as usual. Maren clenched her hand at the thought.

Sherry skipped around the table on one foot. "Yes, but somebody else."

"Of course, but who?"

Sherry stopped and fixed her mother with earnest eyes. "I want to invite Tony."

"Tony? Tony Mountforth?" Something inside Maren gave a hop.

"Tony with the special melon spoon, Mommy. You know! Can I invite him?"

"But . . ." Maren didn't want to explain why Tony shouldn't be invited. "Em. I . . . I think he works in the evening."

"Yes. At the restaurant, I know. You should take me too. You said he gives you ice cream every time you go to see him. Why don't you take me along?"

"Because it's work, honey, it's not fun."

"You go there all the time." Sherry sounded as if Maren invented the meetings to get more ice cream.

"It's because we're preparing a speech. And when you prepare a speech with two people, you have to study exactly who is going to speak at which moment. It's a bit like your dance."

Sherry nodded. After a while, she said, "And he gives you ice cream every time?"

Maren smiled. "Yes. Or a fruit cocktail." She didn't admit that each meeting with Tony made her so nervous, she could only remember with difficulty what she had eaten.

Sherry climbed onto her lap and started to stroke Maren's face. "Please, Mommy, dear, dear Mommy, can you take me along?"

"No, darling, it would distract me, and I wouldn't be able to work. Besides, we've almost finished. There is only one more meeting on Monday." A gloomy thought. Maren pushed it away.

"But I could be very, very quiet, like a little mouse,

and eat a little ice cream, and I promise I wouldn't disturb you and . . ."

"No! Why do I always have to say things a million times?"

Sherry sighed. Seeing her woebegone face, Maren suppressed a smile. At least they had dropped the subject of inviting Tony to the dance. "Shall we have an ice-cream party on Sunday, then?"

Sherry clapped her hands. "Yes! We will make chocolate chip and melon ice cream!"

Maren drew a deep breath. "Sure. Do you want to invite Carol?"

"Yes. No. I don't know."

"All right." Maren frowned in thought. "Or maybe you want to invite Cathy or . . . how about Bridget? Bridget ate three batches of ice cream the last time she came. She loved it."

Sherry chewed her lip and frowned. She stared into space without replying. Then, she pulled herself up and said in an official-sounding voice, "I'll let you know." She threw her mother a defiant glance out of the corner of her eyes. "That's what you always say on the phone."

Maren laughed. "Okay. Let me know when you have made up your mind, Ms. Christensen."

Chapter Ten

"Tony's restaurant, good evening. You're speaking to Belinda Honor."

Silence.

"Hello?"

"Hello." The voice sounded squeaky. "I . . . I want to speak to Tony, please."

"Yes, of course. Hold on a minute." Belinda put the call through to Tony's office.

"Yes, Belinda?"

"A child wants to speak to you."

"A child?" Tony frowned.

"Yeah."

"Don't you think it's for Giovanni?"

"Definitely not. Chiara and I are quite chummy now. Will you take her?"

"Sure." Tony shook his head. Which child could want to speak to him? He decided to drop the official greeting and said, "Hi, this is Tony speaking."

"Hel-Hello Tony, I want to invite you to our ice-cream party."

Tony sat up straight. "Sherry? Is this Sherry?"

"Yes, of course." Sherry sounded affronted that he had not recognized her voice immediately. "Will you come?"

Tony blinked. Did Maren know? "I . . . I'd love to come, Sherry. Thank you for the invitation. When is the party?"

"On Sunday. We will have melon ice cream. Mom made her own recipe."

So Maren did know. Was it a sign she was finally thawing? "That sounds delicious. What time should I come?"

"Mommy said in the afternoon. At . . . three." It sounded as if Sherry had just made up her mind that three was a good time.

He had to get someone else to do his shift. "All right, I'll be there. Thank you for the invitation, Sherry."

Long after Sherry had hung up, Tony stared at the receiver. Had he heard her correctly? Had they invited him to their home? It sounded as if they were friends. And yet, nothing, nothing at all had led him to suspect that Maren had softened toward him. On the contrary, she kept him at arm's length, had never mentioned a possible meeting on Sunday when they had fixed their last date for the Monday afterward. What on earth had made her change her mind?

Maren took the bottle of milk out of the fridge and gave it to Sherry. "Have you already invited somebody for our ice-cream party on Sunday, Sherry? You said you wanted to let me know."

Sherry bent her head and concentrated on filling her cereal bowl with milk. "Yes, Mommy. It's all done. We'll have a surprise guest."

"Ah." Maren smiled at the pigtails below her. How sweet she was. She must have overheard her discussion with Granny yesterday, organizing a surprise party for Annie next month. "And you won't tell me anything? Can't I guess?"

"No." Finally, Sherry lifted her head and grinned. "I won't breathe a word."

"Ohhh, how unfair." Maren dropped onto her chair next to Sherry. "Will the guest eat a lot of ice cream?"

"Yes." Sherry opened her mouth as if to add something, then closed it again with a snap.

Maren suppressed a smile and couldn't resist to give her a quick kiss, just to feel the softness of Sherry's cheek. She was certain Bridget would be the guest because Sherry had asked for her number yesterday. Besides, Carol and her parents had gone out of town for the weekend so they couldn't be invited. "Fine. Then we'd better plan an extra batch." She grinned at her daughter. "Hurry up now, love, or you'll miss the school bus."

Maren had just waved good-bye to Sherry in the school bus when a car stopped at the curb. "Annie!" Maren opened her front door wide. "What a nice morning surprise. Where do you spring from?"

"I've just finished my night shift. Had to work overtime today." Annie hugged Maren. "When I realized I was late enough to scrounge a coffee off you, I decided on a whim to drop by."

Maren looked at her. Annie had circles beneath her eyes and seemed pale. "Of course," she said. "Come and join me. The coffee is ready."

"What a quirky house you have," Annie said. "I've never yet seen a front door that leads immediately into the kitchen."

Maren laughed. "I believe the house was designed to fill a slim hole in a row of several houses. Have a look around, if you want. It won't take long. Behind the kitchen is the living room. It leads straight into our garden. That's the best part about it."

Annie poked her head into the living room. "Where do those stairs lead to?" Maren poured a steaming cup of coffee and pushed the sugar bowl next to it. Then she joined Annie and pointed upstairs. "It ends in my bedroom on the second floor. Right above the kitchen is the bathroom."

"And Sherry?"

"Sherry owns the third and last floor of the house, right beneath the roof. It has slanted walls. She loves it."

Annie nodded. "I won't go up there today; I'm too tired. Where does that lovely coffee smell come from?"

They returned to the kitchen. Annie dropped into her chair, took a sip of coffee, and closed her eyes. "Ahh. That feels good. Well, at least you won't get varicose veins with all those stairs."

Maren laughed. "I never thought about that. But I won't tell my landlord or he'll raise the rent."

"How on earth did you manage with your sprained ankle?"

"It was all right. I hopped like a handicapped grasshopper, and Sherry was a great help. She ran up and down all the time to fetch me things." Maren took out the milk from the fridge and put it on the table. "My ankle is much better now. I barely feel it anymore."

Annie looked at her. "Why did you move away from your parents?"

Maren poured herself a coffee, added milk, and sat down. She inhaled the creamy mocha fragrance and felt the steam touch her cheeks. "I had to live my own life. I'm almost thirty, you know, and it was high time I started living on my own." She smiled. "Maybe I should say restart. After all, I already lived with Brad, but when Sherry was born and I had to move back to my parents', it felt like leaving all independence behind."

"I see." Annie smiled at her, the wrinkles on her face deepening. "That reminds me . . . how is the leopard?"

Maren could feel herself going red. "Em . . . Would you like some more coffee?"

"Yes, please. You know, I thought he was charming."

Maren sat up straight. She had to tell Annie the truth. It was funny with Annie, even if she hadn't seen her for months and months, and in spite of their age gap, the minute they met, they were back on the same level of friendship as they were when they lived next door and saw each other every day. She grabbed Annie's cup and filled it. "The one you met is indeed charming. But that was his twin."

Annie blinked. "Excuse me?"

Maren had to laugh in spite of herself. "Chris Mountforth planted his twin brother with me that night at the restaurant. I have no clue why; maybe he couldn't stomach being with me for several uninterrupted hours; maybe he had something better to do." She bit her lips. "I . . . I think I told you I didn't care for Chris. But I was immediately attracted to Tony. That's the twin, you know. He owns the restaurant where we had dinner."

Annie's eyes grew wide. "Tony's Restaurant? I know it. It's the best restaurant on the island, first class, in fact."

"Yeah." Maren nodded. "Right after dinner, I saw through the masquerade. I felt so cheated and . . . and stupid. I wanted to take my revenge immediately, and so I asked him to spend more time with me. He took me to his boat." She grinned. "All the time on his boat, I talked business. He was lost, of course. But I felt like a louse in the end and asked him to take me home. That's when I sprained my ankle. It's Tony you know, not Chris."

Annie whistled. "What a story."

"Hmm. He called me later and asked me to work with him on a project—no, two, in fact."

Annie smiled. "So the leopard hasn't changed his spots, but he has a brother without any. I'm glad you're happy."

Maren blinked. "No, no, you got that wrong. I'm not going out with Tony."

Annie's shrewd eyes assessed her. "Aren't you?"

Maren swallowed. "Not at all. I don't need a man who lies to me the second he meets me."

"Hmm." Annie drank from her cup without taking her gaze off Maren. "And if he hadn't lied to you that night, would it have made a difference?"

Something hot ran through Maren. "I . . . oh. It . . . it might. But I don't need a man right now." She made a move with her arm as if to wipe away the idea. "I don't have the time; I don't have the energy."

Annie smiled. "That's usually the best time to meet a man. It's only when you wait for them that you never seen 'em."

Maren swallowed. "Sherry adores him but she has no clue what a change it would be. And what if . . . what if . . ." She fell silent and stared into her empty cup.

"What if?" Annie's voice was gentle.

"What if he's like Brad? What if he feels trapped as soon as we're married? What if he decides he doesn't feel ready to be a father and leaves as soon as I become pregnant?"

"Brad wasn't mature enough. You had just finished university, don't forget that."

"Brad is as old as I am," Maren said.

Annie smiled. "But he was way out of his depth." She tilted her head to one side. "Tony, however, knows exactly what he's doing."

"Yeah." Maren's voice sounded bitter. "And he'll know exactly when he wants to leave again. Then I'll have to pick up the broken pieces, and this time, Sherry will be older and will feel it so much more."

Annie put her hand onto Maren's arm. "Listen, dear. At one point in your life, you will have to decide if you dare to trust again, or if you want to let the old pain win. It's up to you."

"How can I trust a man who lies to me and never even admits it?" Maren bent forward and balled her fists. "If he told me about it, I would be able to forget it. But he pretends it never happened!"

Annie frowned. "Hmm. You're right, that's not good. I can't explain it either."

"See?"

"Nevertheless, follow your instincts, follow your gut feeling."

Maren snorted and shook her head. "My gut feeling

tells me only one thing. Run . . . anywhere but into his arms."

The July sky arched hazy blue over Bainbridge Island. Maren and Sherry spent the morning preparing the ice cream so it could churn in the ice-cream machine until the afternoon.

At two o'clock, it got so hot that Maren took a quick shower, threw on an old halter top and a pair of cutoff jeans. She twisted her hair into a knot and fixed it on top of her head. As she looked into the mirror, she wondered if she should make up her face, but decided against it. It was too much hassle and only two little girls would see her today; two little girls who were entirely busy with ice cream and their games.

Back in the kitchen, Maren opened the front door a crack just in case Bridget arrived the minute they were in the garden.

"It's a purrfect, purrfect day for a party!" Sherry sang as she hopped on one leg through the kitchen. "Can we make a picnic and sit on my rug in the garden?"

"Yes, why not." Maren figured that the girls would soon play alone, leaving her a chance to finish the presentation on her laptop. "Do you know where to find the rug?"

"Yes, yes, yes." Sherry picked up a chair and carried it to the built-in cupboard that stored everything from Christmas tree bulbs to Easter bunnies, from ski boots to snorkels. She vanished inside and Maren heard her sing, muffled now, "It's a purrfect, purrfect day for a party."

Maren smiled to herself. She had to learn to appreciate the small moments. Really, she worried too much. She picked up another melon and turned, then froze.

Tony Mountforth stood in the door of her kitchen, smiling at her. The melon dropped from Maren's grip and exploded at her feet. It spattered her bare legs, the kitchen floor, the chair, and all cupboards with red bits of melon and juice.

Maren closed her eyes. Surely she had dreamed him up? Did these things happen? She opened them again.

He still stood there, his smile gone. "I'm sorry, I didn't want to scare you. The door wasn't closed, and I heard your voices. I knocked, but nobody heard me."

Maren wanted to say something, but the words got stuck in her mouth. Sherry shot out of the cupboard like a frenzied ghost and slithered toward him, then threw herself into his arms.

Maren blinked. It wasn't like Sherry to hug total strangers.

Tony hugged her as if he was used to it and released her with a grin. "Thank you for the invitation."

Sherry's eyes met Maren's, her gaze triumphant.

The little witch. Maren grabbed her voice from somewhere out of her stomach and managed a croak. "Welcome."

He stretched out his hand and held up a bag. "I've brought some waffles and gummy bears to decorate the ice cream. But maybe we should first clear up the mess?"

Sherry dived into the bag. "Is it something for me?"

"Sherry! Please wait." Maren wanted to catch her hands, but she stood in a pool of melon juice and didn't want to slip and end up on her rear end in front of the best-looking man who'd ever entered her kitchen.

Two minutes later, they were all on their knees, wiping the floor. *I don't believe it.* Maren stole a look at Tony across the floor. *She set us up!* At that instant, he glanced up and smiled at her, as if they were conspirators in a game. She felt her face going red and averted her eyes.

Sherry distributed melon juice with vigor all along a cupboard front and snickered. "Heh, heh, you didn't guess, did you, Mommy?"

Oh, no. She had to stop her. Maren said, "You have to wash your sponge in clear water, otherwise you only make it worse, Sherry."

"Yes, but you didn't guess! It was a complete surprise!"

Tony wrung out his cloth in the sink. "What was a surprise?"

"Nothing," Maren said. "Shall we look into the bag now, Sherry?"

But it was too late. "Mommy didn't know you were coming!" Sherry beamed at Tony.

Tony whipped around. "What? You didn't know I was coming?"

"Er. No." Maren smiled at him as if she had a toothache and joined him at the sink to wash her sponge.

"I'm sorry." His voice sounded rough. "Should I go?"

Maren turned her head. Her eyes locked with his. His smile had faded, and a white line in the corner of his mouth showed he'd pressed his lips together.

In the background, Sherry jumped up. "Nooo, no, don't go, Tony!"

Maren cleared her throat. "Please stay."

He still looked as if someone had hit him, and all at once, nothing was more important than to wipe away that look from his face. "I'd be happy if you stayed," Maren said.

He frowned. "You're being polite."

Maren swallowed. For no reason at all, her heart raced. "No. I'm being honest."

"Look, Mommy, I can turn out little melon balls just as perfect as Tony."

Maren smiled. "Yes, my love. You'll end up a prime melon-ball-maker."

She exchanged a look with Tony who had stretched himself out on the rug, his arms crossed behind his head. The leaves of the birch tree above threw a dappled shadow over them. It made her nervous to see him so relaxed next to her; she was not used to have sexy men so close.

"You couldn't have bought Sherry a better gift," she said.

"If someone loves a gift as much as that, it's fun to offer it," he said. "The last time I tried a special gift, it was a flop."

"What did you give?" Sherry asked.

Maren was glad Sherry was as curious as herself.

"A birthday dinner."

Maren couldn't stop herself. "What? You offered a birthday dinner, and . . . and it was a flop? Why?"

He sat up and rubbed his forehead. "I should have known it in advance, but sometimes, well . . ." He smiled a lopsided grin. "I offered to cook dinner at my father's birthday, for about twenty guests. He was horrified."

"Horrified?"

Tony shrugged. "Yeah, he thinks everybody who works in a kitchen is on a par with the guys who sweep the street for a living."

Maren swallowed.

Tony smiled at Sherry. "Tell me about your school dance. Do you have your costume here?"

"Yes!" Sherry jumped up. "I'll show you." She dropped the melon spoon and ran into the house.

Maren laughed. "Now you've set her off. She can't wait for that dance. How did you know about it?"

"She told me once, when I called you."

"Hmm." Maren wanted to stretch out too, but she didn't dare. He might lie down again. It would be too intimate, to lie next to him, even if it was on the grass, in full view of her daughter. She crossed her legs and started to scratch at a little red spot. "I still have bits of melon sticking to my legs," she said.

His grin was rueful. "I'm sorry I scared you. How come you didn't know about Sherry's invitation?"

Maren grinned. "Sherry said she would invite a surprise guest, and I guessed wrong." She stole a look at him. His blue eyes searched her face, a bit insecure. She took a deep breath. "But I couldn't have made a better choice."

There. She'd said it. To hide her nervousness, she bent forward, picked up the melon spoon Sherry had dropped and wiped it clean on a tissue. The silence between them lengthened. Butterflies started to dance inside Maren. She had to talk about something to bridge the silence. Anything. "I wanted to discuss something with you, about our meeting with Mr. Brown. I thought it might be good if we showed the layout of your restaurant on the data projector. You can point out how you planned the interior. It would fit with the part where you describe how many miles a day you run through the restaurant, and how vital it is that everything is accessible in seconds."

She took another deep breath. Thank God for job talk. Nothing like it to regain your composure. Why did he confuse her so much? He was just sitting there, on her rug, doing nothing, nothing at all.

If only he would come a bit closer. Maren jerked back. Had she really thought that? *I wanted to keep him at arm's length*, she reminded herself. *He never told me*

*the truth, though he had plenty of time. I shouldn't for-
get that.* She bit her lips. *Then again, maybe I'm too
strict. He stood in for his brother. Twins are close; they
always help each other. It's understandable. Would I
have preferred him to leave his brother in the mud?*

Maren turned her face toward Tony. Their eyes
locked, and the look in his was so . . . so addictive that
Maren leaned a bit closer. He bent toward her and took
the melon ball spoon out of her hands, gently, yet firmly.
As his fingers touched hers, a delicious shiver ran down
her spine. She could feel her lips curve in an involun-
tary smile.

His hand came up, and with one finger he traced her
cheek. Maren didn't dare to move, hardly dared to
breathe. The warmth of his fingertip made her skin tingle
with pleasure. Moving in slow motion, not wanting to
break the spell, she leaned closer. He smelled of melon
and a subtle aftershave she couldn't place. Grapefruit?

In spite of herself, her eyes closed. She lifted her
face to his and waited for his lips to touch hers.

The back door banged.

Maren jerked back.

Sherry shot out of the house and skipped toward
them, her long green-pink dress fluttering around her.

Maren clenched her fists. She felt as if someone had
grabbed a gift from her hands.

Sherry shouted across the garden, "I'm Annabel,
Tony. I'm a flower, and Carol is a flower, and we are in
the garden where the sheep dance, and we dance too."

She turned on her toes until her skirt flared out. "Look, Tony, it's nice, isn't it?"

Maren watched him as he replied. His eyes laughed whenever Sherry said something funny, but he didn't treat her in a condescending way. No wonder Sherry had fallen for him.

And no wonder she had fallen for him too. There. She had admitted it. Why hadn't Sherry arrived two minutes later? She knew she would lie awake all night and relive that moment.

Chapter Eleven

"Nice to meet you, Mr. Brown."

"Nice to meet you, Ms. Christensen." Craigh Brown dropped Maren's hand and gripped Tony's with a beaming smile. "Tony Mountforth! I'm pleased to see you again. If all our pupils were as successful as you are, I could double our school fees, har, har, har." He laughed with a sound like a chain-saw.

Maren opened her eyes wide. What a strange man! She shot a look at Tony. A smile quivered in the corner of his mouth. She had to look away and concentrate on the buff brown table in Mr. Brown's office to school her thoughts. If her head started a romantic fantasy every time she looked at his mouth, the presentation was going to be a disaster.

She folded her hands in her lap and tried to concentrate

on Mr. Brown, who had taken down his glasses and polished them. "I thought you could do the presentation in the auditorium," he said. "It'll give you a feel of the place. We've installed a data projector and two microphones this morning, just as you requested."

Without waiting for an answer, he rushed out of the office and led them through echoing hallways that smelled of dust and cleansing agent. Tony looked around him with a reminiscent smile, but Maren had to hold herself back not to clutch his sleeve. She had never liked school, had never liked empty hallways. They seemed so dead, so devoid of feeling. She had counted on a small, cozy meeting in Mr. Brown's office. Darn.

Mr. Brown ushered them through a paneled door into a dark room that smelled as if it had last been used a decade ago, and ever since no oxygen had been allowed in the vicinity. The door closed with a squeak behind them and left them in blue darkness. The sound of Mr. Brown's footsteps disappeared to the right. Then his muffled voice echoed through the room, "Somewhere here's the light switch. I'll have it soon."

Maren took a cautious step forward and bumped into Tony.

"Great place, isn't it?" Tony's soft voice came from somewhere above her.

"Delightful," Maren said, "so cozy."

"Are you nervous?" His breath was warm on her ear, the only human thing around her.

"Hmm."

"Me too. You know, he looks like a plushy owl, but he's sharp. If he doesn't like our presentation, he'll tell us so, not mincing words."

"Thank you," Maren said. "That's all I needed to make me feel better."

Tony chuckled, and she felt his hand clasp hers for a moment. It lifted her heart. At that instant, the light jumped to life, blinding her.

"Har, har, har." The chainsaw laugh filled the room. "Do step up to the platform, please."

Maren pulled herself together and slipped through the aisle, past the mute chairs.

Mr. Brown muttered something and flipped on a few more switches until the platform was flooded in hostile light, and the seating area sank back into musty darkness. His round shape prodded through the aisle and merged into the shadow of a chair somewhere in the first row. "You can begin. Please present it exactly as you would if the auditorium were full."

Right. Maren swallowed. What a setup. She had counted on a bit of small talk and showing the rough concept. She stood frozen.

Tony gripped Maren's arm and led her to the side where a few steps gave access to the platform. He switched on the projector and tapped his finger against the microphones to check if they worked. The sound echoed through the empty auditorium. Meanwhile, Maren hurried to unpack her laptop and opened their file. She worked as fast as she could, feeling Mr. Brown's presence just a few feet from her as if he was tapping his wrist-watch. Oh, how she wished she had a some gummy bears, to soothe her nerves a bit.

At last, they were ready. Tony gripped his microphone. "Welcome to today's presentation, 'How to Set Up Your Own Restaurant.' I'm Tony Mountforth, owner of Tony's Restaurant on Bainbridge Island . . ."

Maren smiled at him and continued, hoping her voice would sound less wobbly than she felt. "And I'm Maren Christensen, owner of The Start-Up Company. I'm a consultant, and I help people to set up their own businesses."

She stopped to take a breath, and as arranged, Tony took over. "Mr. Brown invited us today to tell you about the beginnings of Tony's Restaurant . . ."

". . . and all the pitfalls you can avoid with a good concept when shaping up your dream and creating your own restaurant," Maren added. Her voice gained strength, and as the familiar words came back, she gained confidence. Thank God Tony had insisted on all their preparatory meetings.

Tony continued with a smile Maren found irresistible. It would lift half the female audience off their seats. "You will soon realize that I didn't prepare well, and boy, did I pay for it." Tony grinned at Maren.

She grinned back. His last sentence had not been part of their script, but it felt fine, robbing his words of any preachy effect they might have had. Maybe they were a good team on stage. Maren felt the blood rushing up to her face. To hide it, she bent forward to click onto the keyboard of her laptop to reveal the next page of their presentation.

The next hour passed in a blur. With each word they said, the presentation gained momentum. The Mountforth charm was in full effect; in fact, Maren found it hard to avert her gaze from Tony. But maybe that was all right. It wouldn't do to look bored when he spoke, would it? When they finished, Maren took a deep breath and drew a hand through her hair. She was hot and happy, buoyed up by all the adrenaline. That was it. She had done all she could, now she could only pray that Mr. Brown liked it.

A single pair of hands clapped below them, making such a lonely sound that Maren wished he would stop. "Brilliant." Mr. Brown's voice floated up out of the darkness. He didn't sound as if they had swept him off his feet; on the contrary, he sounded dry, a bit ironic even.

Maren clutched the microphone harder. He was probably looking for kind words to say he was only interested in having Tony speak. After all, that's what he had wanted from the start, nothing else. Oh, how she wanted to do the presentation, even if it meant she had to do something drastic. Not only because it meant spending time with Tony (she tried not to measure the extent of this motivation), but also because they had created something good together, something that might push both their careers forward. She tried to take a deep breath, but the dry air rasped her throat, and she had to cough.

The voice below said, "Can you do the presentation on the twenty-third?"

Maren threw a wild look at Tony. Had she heard correctly? Had they really made it? She wanted to jump up and down and punch the air.

"The twenty-third?" Tony said with a calm voice as if he had never doubted the outcome. "That's Friday already, isn't it?"

"Yes."

Maren froze. *Oh, no.* This Friday. On Friday she had the Henry Barker meeting at three in the afternoon and Sherry's dance in the evening. Why did things always come in clusters?

"Would . . . would the twenty-second also be possible?" she asked.

"I'm afraid not." Mr. Brown's disembodied words floated through the stale air. Against the glaring lights, Maren couldn't even make out his shape. It felt as if she was having a discussion with a ghost. "The twenty-third is the last day of term, and we've already booked all the classes into the auditorium. Mr. Mountforth will remember that it's a tradition to hold a special speech every year."

"I do," Tony said, "but in general, the speaker was chosen well in advance, wasn't he?"

"Indeed he was, but he happened to hug a lamp post when he went in-line skating four weeks ago. He's still in a cast." There wasn't the slightest smile in Mr. Brown's voice.

Maren suppressed a hysterical giggle. "When would the speech begin?" she asked.

"At ten a.m."

At ten in the morning. She might make it. She might be able to cram three world-shaking events into just one day. And after Sherry's dance, she would finish the evening with a heart attack. "It's fine for me," Maren said, her voice as firm as she could make it.

"You were brilliant." The wind blew Tony's dark hair out of his face. A wave of exhaust streamed past them as the ferry cast off and started to chug toward Bainbridge Island.

Maren smiled. "Funny. I thought *you* were."

His blue-green eyes looked at her. "So maybe we're a good team?"

Her heart made a funny skip and ended up in her throat. "Maybe we are."

He bent closer. "For sure we are."

Without allowing herself to think, Maren lifted her hand and caressed the short hair at the nape of his neck with her fingertips. What a delicious feeling. "For sure." Her voice was a whisper. And then, his lips covered hers, and for a crazy instant, Maren wondered if she would fall overboard because everything rocked, but the next moment, his arms encircled her, strong and warm, and she knew she was safe.

"Well, well, well," a voice behind them said.

Maren emerged from the embrace as if coming back from another world. She blinked and stared, then swallowed. Her hand gripped the railing.

"Hi." Tony sounded as if he spoke through clenched teeth.

Chris smiled. "I saw you from the other side of the boat and thought I'd come over."

Maren opened her mouth, but nothing came out. She looked from Chris to Tony. Same tilt of eyebrows, same curve of jaw. And yet, so different.

Tony leaned with his back against the railing and looked at his brother, his face inscrutable.

"Did you have a nice day?" Chris ignored the vibes.

"Yeah, thanks." Tony's voice could have cut ice.

Maren couldn't stand it anymore. Her knees felt like pudding, and her stomach made queasy motions. "I'll get back into the car," she said. "It's too windy." She nodded at Chris and fled.

"Well, Tony?" Chris drew out the words. "Who did she think she was kissing? You or me?"

Tony took a deep breath. Why did Chris have to show up? He sighed. "Maren wouldn't kiss you."

Chris laughed. "Want to take a bet?"

"No." Tony closed his mouth with a snap. A seagull shrieked as if it was making fun of him. "I introduced myself to Maren under my own name." He forced himself to remain calm. "And I never talked to her about the other night. Although it cost me."

"Ha. You want me to believe that?"

"I do. What's more, I want to tell her the truth, though I believe she guessed it a long time ago."

Chris shook his head and leaned against the ferry's rail. "You're still not making sense, Tony. If she had guessed the truth, she wouldn't kiss you. I can guarantee that. On the other hand, if she hasn't guessed, then all's well. Why stir up trouble?"

Tony threw a look toward his car. Maren had closed the door and stared in the other direction. Something inside him hurt. "I know her better, and I know it would be right to tell her."

Chris sighed. "You're so pigheaded sometimes, Tony." Then he lifted his hands. "All right. You can tell her anything you want, but don't involve me."

Tony crossed his arms in front of his chest. "Great. That doesn't get me anywhere, and you well know it."

Chris bent forward and grabbed Tony's arm. "Listen, brother, that woman is bad news. I know it. She told Dad I'm a loser, and thanks to her, he made a scene worse than the one when you wanted to become a cook."

"She didn't tell Dad anything of the kind."

Chris pulled himself up. "She didn't? How can you say she didn't? Were you there? Were you—"

"Yes."

"What do you mean, yes?"

"I overheard their conversation when she told him she had found another tax consultant. The worst she said was that you didn't see eye to eye."

"See?" Chris narrowed his eyes. "That's what I mean. She seems so cool and controlled, but underneath, she makes those poisonous digs."

Tony felt hot fury rising inside him. "For heaven's sake! She didn't make any poisonous digs! She kept on neutral ground as long as she could."

"Oh, yeah? I don't believe a word. It seems she has you infatuated. Well, good luck with the iceberg. Rather you than me."

Tony fought down his irritation. "What did Dad say to you?"

"Say?" Chris frowned. "He didn't say anything. He whispered. You know what it's like when he starts to whisper. He said I was a smudge in the company history. He said I was useless."

Tony bit his lips. "Chris . . ."

"What now?"

"If . . . if you could start again. If . . . if Dad hadn't marked the way already. What would you do?"

Chris pushed himself away from the rails. "Tony, you're getting on my nerves. I wish you happiness with the iceberg. But don't complain if it gets too cold." He turned away, then over his shoulder he said, "By the way, if she has guessed the truth, then her kisses might be part of an elaborate plan of revenge. Beware, my brother."

* * *

Maren shot a quick look at Tony as he threw himself into the car. He was pale and tight-lipped. What on earth had Chris said to him? She averted her gaze. What could she say to break up the tension? She hunted for the right words, but her brain refused to work.

Tony cleared his throat. Without looking at her, he said, "I liked your first report about the jetty project. I read it yesterday afternoon."

Maren's heart collapsed into her stomach. At least that's how it felt. How could he try to talk business now? How could he kiss her, turn around, and discuss figures? Could he turn his heart on and off like a flashlight? Why didn't he trust her? Why didn't he tell her the truth?

She swallowed and opened her mouth, but nothing came out.

Tony stared straight ahead. His voice sounded strange. "Even though it's more expensive, I like a wooden jetty better than concrete. But I wondered if wood wouldn't be too slippery when it's wet."

Maren balled her hands. She didn't want to discuss business. She wanted him to stop at the side of the road, tell her the truth, and kiss her again.

Now pull yourself together, Maren. This is your biggest project. Answer him! Maren took a deep breath. "I'll ask them about it." Her voice sounded like a foreign thing, flat and dead.

"Thanks."

Maren turned her back to him and stared out the side window with unseeing eyes. He didn't try to strike up another conversation until, an eternity and two days later, he sat her down at her front door.

"I'm sorry," he said the instant she got out of his car.

Maren didn't reply. She ran to her house, rushed through the door, shut it behind her and burst into tears.

Just as she had managed to overcome her scruples. Just as she had dared to be happy. Why did Chris have to show up? Why did he make a scene?

It wouldn't have mattered if only Tony had explained it to her. But after that inane sentence about the jetty, he had remained mute, as if she wasn't there at all.

It hurt. Oh, how it hurt. All the special feeling gone; the feeling that had made her believe they belonged together. Maren hid her face in her hands. Thank God Sherry was still in school; at least she wouldn't see her mother cry like a lost five-year-old. She stumbled upstairs into the bathroom and grabbed a towel to wipe her face, but the more she tried to control herself, the more tears came.

She had just calmed down enough to go to the kitchen and make herself a cup of coffee when the phone rang. Maren swallowed and said, "The Start-Up Company" to the door of the fridge. It sounded much too tearful.

The phone rang again. Maren straightened and bellowed, "The Start-Up Company!" She wouldn't fool anybody with that voice, but she had to answer the phone. It might be a client. Or . . . it might be Tony.

She picked up the receiver. "The Start-Up Company, Maren Christensen speaking."

"Hi, Maren."

Her mother. Maren's clenched muscles collapsed. She dropped into a chair. *How can I cut her short?* "Hi, Mom. How are you?"

"Just fine. Imagine, I met Christobel today in Winslow and she said . . ."

Maren sighed inaudibly. Christobel was Bainbridge Island's number one gossip. "Mom, could we talk some other time? I've just returned from a pitch, and I'm drained."

"A pitch? What's a pitch?"

"An interview, the one I told you about, with Tony Mountforth at the Culinary Institute."

"Ah, yes. But that's exactly why I'm calling."

Maren closed her eyes. "Right." Now she was in for it.

"We came to chat a bit, and I mentioned you're going out with Chris Mountforth."

Maren sat up straight. "You mentioned what?"

"Darling, you don't have to be shy about it. I know it has been quite some time and—"

"Mom. I am not going out with Chris Mountforth." Maren pronounced each word with care. "I wouldn't dream of it."

Her mother laughed. A light, silvery laugh that reduced Maren's arguments to dust. "Well, anyway, and can you imagine what Christobel said to me? She said the Mountforth twins are bad news."

"Oh, yeah?" Maren clutched the edge of the table.

"Yes. As if she knew anything about it!"

Maren didn't say anything.

Her mother swept on. "She said she could tell me things . . . unsavory, you know."

"Women, drugs, murder?" Maren clenched her teeth.

"There's no need to be sarcastic, dear. Women, mostly. I'm not sure about the other things."

"Well, let her dig some more, and I'm sure she'll turn up something."

"Maren! I don't know what's come over you! I only wanted to tell you so you would be prepared. But of course she's wrong. They're delightful, and it's so amazing how much alike they are. Don't you think?"

"Listen, Mom, I don't want to discuss the Mountforth twins or anything else right now. As I said, I'm exhausted; I need to rest. Good-bye." Maren cut off the connection and threw the phone onto the kitchen table.

Womanizer. Really. As if Tony was a womanizer. It was a different matter with Chris, all right. But that hateful Christobel had talked about the Mountforth twins, hadn't she? How dare she? How . . .

Maren brought herself up short. She had seen a woman in the car next to Tony, on the Sunday after their dinner. They had come from the ferry. Could she have mistaken Chris for Tony? Maren swallowed. No. It had been Tony's white van. Besides, she knew Tony. And she had seen the woman clearly from her father's pickup. A petite woman who reminded her of Saint Madonna with her oval face and her large eyes. Who was she? Tony had never mentioned any woman.

He's not likely to if he makes up to me. Maren shook her head. Where did that nasty thought come from? She wasn't being fair.

He's much too busy for women. Besides, a man has a right to drive a woman around in his car, hasn't he? Why always think the worst?

Maren sighed. *Maybe she was just a friend. I'm acting a bit obsessed here.*

She tried to shrug off the memory, but it remained like a bad taste in her mouth. How could she have forgotten that beautiful woman in Tony's car? She should have trusted her first instincts. Men made trouble. Always.

Most of all, she should never have kissed Tony. Really, what had come over her? Maren pushed away the memory of his arms around her. The smell of his skin had intoxicated her.

No, no. She had no time for men.

Least of all for men who never admitted the truth if it happened to be irksome.

Least of all for men who kissed her, turned around, and talked business.

Despicable.

Chapter Twelve

The all-important day dawned murky. "I hope that's not an omen," Maren said to the dark gray sky as she looked out of her bedroom window.

"What's an omen, Mommy?"

Maren swiveled around. "Gosh, you scared me." She drew her daughter onto her knees. Sherry's cheeks were flushed, her body still warm from sleep. "Good morning, darling. Why are you awake so early?"

Sherry's eyes shone. "Today is the day of the dance."

Maren kissed her. "Yes, I know. Are you excited?"

"Yes! I'm a bit afraid and a bit happy."

Maren laughed. "It's called stage fever."

Sherry hugged her. "Fever? But with fever, you have to stay in bed."

"Well, with this kind of fever, you don't have to."

172

Sherry tilted her head. "You'll come, won't you, Mommy?"

"Yes, of course. I've already promised. Why are you so afraid I won't come?"

Sherry slipped away and hopped to the door without answering. Maren sighed. There were so many things about her daughter she didn't know, so many things going on under the surface. If only Sherry would continue to confide in her. She drew back her shoulders. It had been right to insist on the earlier meeting at Henry Barker Productions, even if it meant being difficult. Some things had preference.

Well, it should be a preference to get food onto the table and clothes onto the girl, shouldn't it? a quarrelsome voice inside her said.

There will always be food. Maren narrowed her eyes. *I can always get a job in an office if my company fails.* She bit her lips. The prospect filled her with dread. Shaking her head to make the scary thought go away, she took out a new pair of gossamer tights. "Don't worry," she said to herself. "I've made it, haven't I? I'll be in time for Sherry's dance, and I have the meeting with Henry Barker. So I can stop whining. Now."

The shrill ring of the phone rent through her thoughts. Who could be calling at twenty past seven in the morning? Her heart clenched. Not an emergency, not today of all days, surely not? Maren lunged for the phone before Sherry, who had shot through the door, could get at it.

"The Start-Up Company, Maren Christensen speaking."

"Hi, darling."

Maren breathed again. "Mom! How come you're calling so early?"

Sherry ran toward her with outstretched arms. "I want to talk to Grandma," she shouted. "Give the phone to me!"

Maren fought her off with a hand. "One minute, Sherry!"

She drew herself up so Sherry couldn't reach the phone. "Mom, Sherry wants to talk to you. I'll pass you on, okay?"

"No, no, wait!" Inga's voice sounded thin and tight.

"What's up?" Maren frowned. Her mother never refused to talk to Sherry. Ever.

"I want to talk to Grandma!" Sherry tugged at Maren's arm.

"Something quite dreadful has happened, and I have to . . ." Inga's last words were drowned out by Sherry's shouting.

Maren glared at her daughter. "Hush up, Sherry! Grandma has to talk to me for a minute."

"But I want . . ." Sherry's voice pierced the room.

Maren turned away from her and went downstairs into the living room. "Yes, Mom, now tell me. What has happened?"

"It's so awful, dear, and I don't know how to tell Sherry, but I really can't help it and . . ."

Maren's stomach coiled into a tight roll. "What has happened?" Her voice sounded sharp and strained.

"Aunt Mary has fallen ill."

"Oh!" Relief flooded Maren. "Aunt Mary. I'm sorry, of course, but after what you said it sounded as if a catastrophe . . ."

"It is a catastrophe," her mother said, "Because she wants us to drive to Spokane right away, and we won't be able to come to Sherry's dance tonight."

Maren grasped the back of a chair to steady her legs. "You won't be able to come to the dance?" she repeated, then wished she had cut off her tongue. She whipped around and stared at the door. Maybe Sherry hadn't heard . . .

But no.

Sherry stood in the door frame without moving, her eyes huge. "Granny and Granddad won't come to my dance?" Her face twisted, then she exploded into sobs.

"Oh, sweetheart." Maren rushed to her and hugged her. "Shhh. Don't cry."

Her mother's voice crackled in her ear.

"I have to call you later, Mom. Make sure you switch on your cell phone so I can reach you, will you? Bye." She threw the phone onto the sofa and drew her daughter into her arms.

"Don't cry, darling. Shh. Don't cry."

"Th-hey—wo-hon't co-ho-home." Sherry's whole body shook.

Maren bit her lips. How to comfort her? "I . . . I think

Mrs. Evans will make a video, and then they can watch it later."

Sherry shook her head. "It wo-ho-hon't be the sa-ha-ame."

No. Of course it wouldn't. "I know." Maren swallowed. Anger surged up inside her. How did the world dare to hurt her daughter? Why did it have to be so unfair? Why did it dare to break her heart when she was still so small? She tried to say something that would help Sherry. "You see, Aunt Mary is ill, and Granny has to go and help her . . ."

Sherry lifted her tear-streaked face. "Who is Aunt Mary? I never heard of her."

Maren sighed. "She's the sister of your great-granddad, and she's very kind and helped Granny a lot when Granny had just arrived in Seattle. Now she needs Granny." She swallowed. "Sometimes people have to do things they don't want to do, you see. Granny has to go although she would prefer to come to your dance."

"I do-hon't care if it's not ni-hice"—Sherry clung to her mother and wiped her nose on Maren's fresh blouse—"bu-hut, I hate Aunt Mary."

Now wasn't the time to say that hate was wrong. Maren hugged Sherry and held her close until the sobbing subsided. When Maren opened her eyes again, her gaze fell on the clock at the wall. They had to hurry. If Sherry missed the school bus, Maren would have to drive her. Then she would be late for the presentation at the Culinary Institute. Sherry was still in her night dress. She had to have breakfast. And Maren had to find another blouse before she left, maybe even iron it.

A shudder made Sherry's body tremble. "Listen, darling," Maren said into the moist little ear, "as soon as we have the video, we'll make a big dance party, and you'll wear your costume again. You can invite Carol too, and we'll all watch the video together. And now, because you are so sad, you can have melon for breakfast!"

Melon for breakfast was a big exception because Sherry had missed the school bus twice because of it and having to re-dress from head to toe. Eating melons was a messy business. "I'll make little melon scoops with your special spoon, and in the meantime, you comb your hair and get dressed, okay?" Maren nudged her daughter toward the stairs.

Sherry shook her head. "No."

"No?"

"I'm not hungry."

"But darling . . ."

Sherry wriggled out of her mother's arms and looked at her, the ends of her mouth tragic, her gaze full of reproach. "How can you think of food when my heart is broken?"

Maren swallowed and gathered Sherry once again into her arms. Then she lifted her up and carried Sherry upstairs, back to her room. "All right. No food this morning. I'll help you dress now." Later, she packed some cornflakes into a Tupperware box and packed them together with an apple into Sherry's bag. Even small girls with broken hearts needed food eventually.

"Hi, Mom."

"Maren! Where are you?"

"I'm on the ferry, on my way to the presentation. And you?"

"We've just hit the Interstate. I'm so sorry about the dance."

"It's not your fault." Maren clenched her phone between her left ear and her shoulder, stretched out her arm, and pulled at her right sleeve. The blouse was too small to be comfortable.

"I hope you understand," her mother said.

"Of course I do. But you can't expect it from Sherry."

"No." Inga's voice sounded weak above the hum of the motor. "How did she take it?"

"Well, you heard her. It took me ages to calm her down. She refused breakfast, and we almost missed the school bus."

"Did you pack her some extra lunch?"

"Yes, of course I did." Maren shook her head. Why did her mother always think she would let Sherry starve?

"You shouldn't have repeated it out loud, you know. It was a bit thoughtless of you."

"Yes." Maren bit her lips and stared at the laden sky.

Everything around her was gray. The sky, the water, her mood.

"If you had thought about your words, you might have told her calmly. It would have lessened the shock."

Maren cringed. "Yes."

"I really don't know why you don't think about your words before you speak. It's easy to say you're sorry afterward, but . . ."

Maren clenched her teeth. "You didn't have the time to tell me anything about Aunt Mary, Mom. You only said she's ill."

"She broke her leg yesterday evening, when she fell down the stairs."

"Oh, dear."

Inga sighed. "Yes. We'll drive straight to the hospital and see what we can do. I'll know more this afternoon, but we have to stay at least one night. Oh, I almost forgot. Could you drive home and water the flowers tonight?"

"Yes, after the dance," Maren said.

"Well, obviously not!" Her mother sounded annoyed. "You don't want to drag your child around in the middle of the night, do you? You can do it before."

"No, I can't." Maren clenched her hand around the phone. "As I've told you, I have a presentation this morning and an important interview in the afternoon. I'll barely manage to make it back in time for the dance, so no time for watering flowers in between."

"You don't need to be snappy just because I once ask you for a favor."

Maren counted to ten, then she said, "I could water them tomorrow morning. Would that do?"

There was a pause, then Inga said, "Well, yes. Let's not fight. I think all our nerves are a bit strained right now."

"You can say that again," Maren said. "Good luck, then. We'll talk this afternoon. Bye, Mom."

She crossed her arms on the roof of her car and dropped her head onto them. Sherry's woebegone face rose before her. No happy good-bye wave this morning; instead, she had climbed into the bus with hanging shoulders. But that wasn't the worst. She had not mentioned her dance again, not even to ask if Maren would be coming. As if she had already accepted that she couldn't rely on the promises of adults. The thought chilled Maren. She lifted her head and stared across the chopping waves, not seeing them. "I'll come to the dance, my sweet," she said through clenched teeth. "I promise."

The auditorium smelled exactly the same, with an added hint of perfume, but today, the audience hummed and rustled like a beehive. As Mr. Brown started his introductory speech, the hum calmed to a whisper. Maren rubbed her clammy hands on her skirt and threw Tony a look. He looked as if he was about to go on vacation, relaxed as ever. But no, now Maren discovered a quick pulse beating at the side of his neck. She drew a deep breath. Thank God he was human too. He turned his head, smiled at her, and bent closer. "I'm going to collapse with nerves in a minute."

"You'll fall on top of me." Her smile felt as if it cracked in her stiff face, but his words helped her.

"And now, dear students, dear teachers." Mr. Brown stood in the spotlight like a moth well accustomed to stardom. "Please welcome Maren Christensen and Tony Mountforth!"

Applause came up so weak, it was obvious the audience was being polite and was not a bit excited. Maren cringed and climbed up the steps to the stage with heavy limbs.

At first, she clung to Tony's smile like a teenager, but after their first three sentences, she felt better. Blinded by the spotlight, she dared to smile into the general direction of the audience and was delighted when she felt the student's interest. The humming sound dropped, and when Tony said his bit about making mistakes, they were ready to laugh. Darlings.

Sweat ran down between her shoulder blades, and her knees had the strength of wet tissue paper, but it didn't matter. She remembered all her lines, and so did he. Once, she got stuck, but he helped her out in such a smooth way nobody noticed. However, the twinkle in his eye did nothing for the stability of her knees.

In no time at all, they neared the end of the presentation, and Tony curved into the final spurt. Maren dared to breathe for the first time and listened to his closing words. "So, no matter what people say, go ahead and realize your dream. It will be hard, no doubt about that. In fact, your parents and friends might not support you . . ." He threw Maren a mischievous glance and took a deep breath. Then he deviated from the script. "Do you want to know what Maren said to me when I told her my profession at our very first meeting?"

Maren jumped.

"She said my job was sizzling hamburgers in a greasy kitchen." Tony turned back to the audience. "And you know it is, sometimes, for a time. But don't be discouraged. Fight for your dream. It's worth it."

He clicked off the microphone, grabbed her hand, and together, they bowed. It was a good thing he pulled her with him, otherwise, Maren would have stood like a stick. Had he really alluded to that dinner she had supposedly had with Chris? Had he said it on purpose or was it a slip of the tongue? She pushed down her thoughts, smiled like a wooden doll, and bowed again. The applause sounded as if they had hit a nerve with the students. A part of her, the part that wasn't confused, laughed with pleasure and relief.

Mr. Brown met them at the foot of the stairs, his glasses dangling from his hand. "Brilliant." He sounded dry as always, and with a scant "good-bye," he vanished into the crowd.

As they worked their way toward the exit, students and teachers stopped them to ask questions and thank them. Maren smiled so hard it ached and tried to give kind and intelligent answers. Somehow, she got separated from Tony. He stayed behind, and out of the corner of her eye, Maren saw a supple beauty stepping into his way. She looked like a sleek birch, all blond and green eyes. He bent his head toward her with alacrity.

Maren tore her gaze away and pressed through the crowd to the auditorium exit. Finally, she reached the double glass doors. It was raining. A steady drizzle moistened the leaves on the trees with a glistening sheen and drenched the street. The smell of wet dust and tarmac billowed through the doors of the auditorium.

Maren knew she had to get away. She would call Tony later. She huddled deeper into her coat, pressed her bag against her chest, and ran across the parking lot.

"Maren, wait!" Tony jumped across a puddle and reached her just as she opened the door of her car.

"I have to go." Maren didn't look at him.

Tony gripped her wrist. "What's wrong? The speech was fantastic. They loved it."

Maren stood rooted to the ground and looked at his hand on her wrist. "Yeah. I know. I'm happy about that."

"So what's wrong? Why did you run away? Did I say anything wrong? Did I . . . ?" he cut himself off and gulped. His hand dropped to his side. "Sizzling hamburgers in a greasy kitchen." His voice sounded rough.

She lifted her head. "Yep."

He stared at her, his blue-green eyes dark like a lake in autumn. For an eternity, neither said anything. The rain rustled onto the leaves, and somewhere it gurgled into a drain.

Finally, Tony drew his hand through his wet hair. "But you knew already, didn't you?"

A drop of rain trickled through Maren's hair and ran down her neck. "Yes, I knew."

"You never let on." His gaze scanned her face.

Water seeped through the thin soles of her shoes, but it didn't matter. "I would have liked you to tell me. Preferably not in front of a hundred people."

He shook his head, dislocating more drops of water in his hair. "I'm sorry. Chris asked me to keep mum."

Maren's stomach coiled up. "And you always obey Chris?"

He sighed. "It was his secret, not mine."

A raindrop loosened from her eyebrow and rolled down to her eyelid until it sat heavy and cold on her lashes. Maren shook her head to get rid of it and crossed her arms in front of her chest. "You may understand, though, that it hurt me. When I found out the game you played . . ."

"When did you find out?"

"The first night. Right after dinner, as we sat in the car."

For a moment, he closed his eyes. "Oh, no. How did you know?"

Maren lifted her foot out of the puddle that had formed around it and took a step to the side. "It's obvious. You're completely different."

He smiled at that, a smile that looked as if a winter morning tried to remember summer. "Funny. Nobody ever said that to me before."

Maren tried to ignore the effect his smile had on her. "I felt cheated . . . and stupid."

"I can imagine. I'm sorry."

Maren stared at him. The rain had found its way through the seams of her rain coat; she could feel her wet blouse clinging to her skin. She had to know. "Why did Chris run away that evening?"

"A friend's computer crashed just before her thesis was due. He rushed over and helped her to reinstall everything."

"Well. It's the first time he had an altruistic reason for standing me up."

"You don't believe me?"

"Not you—I don't believe him."

Tony rubbed his hand across his forehead. "He promised me he would try to improve."

Maren managed a travesty of a smile. "He didn't have a chance. I dropped Mountforth and Adams right afterward."

"I know."

Maren whipped around and opened the door of her car. "Good-bye, Tony."

He grabbed her arm. "Maren. Please don't go. I hated keeping it a secret from you, but I couldn't let Chris down either. I was so torn in two."

"Yes, I understand," Maren said. Well, her head did, to be exact. Her heart was a different matter. If only it didn't hurt so much. "Why . . . why did you suggest breakfast at Annie's house the next day and then didn't come? Was that necessary? I felt so stupid." The memory tightened her throat.

He swallowed. "I couldn't resist, though I knew it was crazy."

"You didn't come."

"I couldn't. I'm not sure if I told you, Guiseppe, my chef, was diagnosed with a bad case of appendicitis that morning."

Maren nodded.

"The hospital called me just as I left the bakery with the cinnamon rolls. Guiseppe insisted on speaking with me before he agreed to the operation."

Maren swallowed. "So you sent Chris instead."

"Yes. I'm sorry. I thought it was better than standing you up yet another time."

What a muddle. Maren had the feeling the air was too thin to breathe. She closed her eyes for an instant. "I have to get a bit of distance right now."

When she opened her eyes, his face was pale and tense, as if she had slapped him.

Maren clenched her teeth. "Besides, it's wet. Bye."

She turned on her heels, dove into her car, threw the door shut, and started the motor. As she turned out of the parking lot, she allowed herself one look into the rearview mirror. He stood without moving in the rain, and stared after her.

Chapter Thirteen

Maren had intended to find an Internet café and spend the remaining time there before her Henry Barker interview, but she felt so cold and wet and miserable that she decided to drive home. She would just have the time to rush in and right out again, but at least she wouldn't arrive like a wet dog at her interview. Her self-confidence needed every possible prop to face the TV people.

She turned into Madison Street and slammed on the brakes. The road was jammed. A horn blared somewhere and a scarlet-faced driver in a green Honda next to her banged a fist onto his dashboard. Up front, nothing moved. Maren threw a look into the rearview mirror. Could she reverse and get out? No, a truck chugged an inch behind her. It blocked her road to escape. She could do nothing but wait.

Her hair dripped, and her feet felt numb with cold. Maren switched on the heater. How she wished she had a towel to dry her hair. She rummaged in her bag and unearthed a picture of a crooked house (courtesy of Sherry), a half-eaten candy partly wrapped in its paper (ditto), her lipstick, soaked tissues, an old receipt for gas, and the business card of a man she couldn't remember. The only useful things were two extra pairs of shoes.

Maren frowned. She had to stock up on an emergency kit, like, for starters, a towel, some basic food, Band-Aids, and most important of all, white gummy bears to soothe her nerves. Her stomach grumbled. She'd been too nervous and stressed to eat anything for breakfast. To her right, a Café Madison advertised bagels with cream cheese. Maren clutched the steering wheel and dragged her gaze away from the poster. How much longer was she going to sit here, condemned to immobility? She checked the time. With every minute, the likelihood of catching the ferry receded. Maybe she should forget about her car, get out, and buy a bagel to go. But of course the traffic would pick up the second she was inside the café. Or would it? Maren frowned. Her stomach grumbled. She threw another look at the poster with the bagel. Her mouth watered. Oh, what the heck.

Maren threw open the door of her car, grabbed her handbag, jumped out, and ran into the café. The sweet smell of pastry and coffee enveloped Maren like an embrace. She drew a deep breath and looked toward the counter. Just one customer to be served before her. Perfect. The woman behind the counter sported a cluster of tight curls and an apron in an alarming shade of red. As she welcomed the lady before Maren, a smile blossomed on her face, broad and slow. "Good day, ma'am, what can I do for you?" She pronounced each word with care.

The customer, a fragile-boned lady who barely reached Maren's shoulders, tittered. "I'm not quite sure today," she said, leaned onto her walking stick, and peered through the glass front at the display.

Maren shifted her weight from one foot to the other. She eyed the bagels like a lion assessing a gazelle.

Another titter from the old lady. "What do you recommend?"

Maren swiveled on her heels and threw a haunted look at her car. The traffic was still blocked. Nothing moved. Good. She swiveled back and dug out her purse. No change left, just a fifty dollar bill. It meant another delay when paying.

"Weeeell." The lady with the curls leaned against the display and observed the pastries as if seeing them for the first time. "The cream puffs are delicious."

The tiny lady tittered again. Her brown coat made her look like a sparrow. "Oh, no," she said. "I'm afraid I can't eat cream puffs." She leaned forward. "Indigestion, you know," she whispered.

The curly-haired lady nodded in grave understanding.

Maren's stomach twisted in pain. She shifted her weight again, checked on the traffic—still blocked—crossed her arms, and tapped her fingers. Surely they wouldn't discuss all kinds of illnesses now?

"How about a bagel?" the service lady suggested, moving an inch per minute toward the pile of bagels to her left. "We have a special offer for the ones with sesame."

Maren wanted to throw her money onto the counter, grab a bagel, and run to the door. It took all her self-control to remain standing, if that's what it could be called when she was hopping up and down with nerves.

"Sesame?" The sparrow sighed and shook her head. "No, you see, I have an allergy to sesame."

The curly-haired woman looked as if someone had died. "Oh, no. How sad. Sesame is so healthy."

At that instant, Maren's stomach grumbled so loud, she was sure everybody had heard it. Her head felt dizzy, and that delicious, delicious smell filled her senses until she was all but inebriated. She crumpled the fifty dollar note in her hands and threw a look over her shoulder. Did the traffic start to move? Her heart stopped. Did it? Something seemed to move up front. She whipped around, lifted herself onto her toes, and craned her neck.

No. Not yet. Thank God. Behind her, the conversation continued.

"But I like poppy seed," the sparrow now said.

Maren turned back to them with a sigh.

In slow motion, the shop assistant shook her head and lifted her hand to her cheek. "I'm afraid we don't have anything with poppy seed."

That did it. Maren bent forward, "Excuse me, please, I'm in a bit of a hurry. Could you please pass me just one bagel? I'd very much appreciate that."

Major mistake.

Both women froze and stared at her in consternation.

"I have almost chosen," the sparrow replied with dignity, then muttered, "Really, the young people today have strange manners," before she concentrated once again on the display.

Maren almost broke into tears. She bit her lips and stared at the floor. She was so hungry. So hungry. Maybe she could grab the bagel next to her elbow and eat it right away, before paying for it.

No, that would scandalize the lady so much, it would result in her imminent arrest. She threw a look at the assistant who was now discussing the advantages of apple pie with every sign of enjoyment.

If only she had a gummy bear to chew. She checked on her car. The driver of the green Honda had gotten out and stood in the open door with his elbow on his roof, frowning at something invisible in the distance. Good.

The discussion between the ladies proceeded. Apple pie it was.

Maren drew a deep sigh of relief.

The curly-haired assistant wrapped up the precious

piece of apple pie as if it was a baby. The time it took to hand it over, get out the purse, count the change, and say loving farewells would have allowed Maren to dress and undress three times. With another reproachful glance, the sparrowlike lady hobbled past Maren.

Now.

Her turn.

Maren took a step forward and smiled. "I'd like a—"

A horn blasted out behind her, then another. Maren whipped around.

"My goodness." The curly-haired lady shook her head. "There seems to be a car abandoned in the middle of the road. Really, some people . . ."

Maren didn't hear the rest of the sentence. She ran out the door and narrowly missed being run over by the cars that shot past hers, standing immobile like an island in a thunderous sea.

She missed the ferry.

Resigned, she decided to find a little café but spent half an hour looking for a parking space. In the end, she had to make do with a rundown little spot on a side street. Exhausted, she retreated into the bathroom. A woman with a wild expression in her eyes and hair like a witch stared back from the mirror. The dried water on her jacket had left whitish rims on her best suit. She looked like a sewer rat.

Maren set to work with the meager material she had at hand. With a tissue and infinite care, she started to rub the mud splashes off her tights. Just as she tackled the last spot, her fingernail got hooked and ripped a ladder into it. Faster than she could look, it ran all the way to her ankle. Maren suppressed an oath. Who had invented tights anyway? A sadistic man?

Thank God she had brought spare tights. Maren fished them out of her bag and eased into them. Then she saw it. A hole, large as a fist, just below her knee. She stared at it. Yesterday, they had been perfect, without the tiniest fault. She crumpled them in her hands. "Don't cry." She spoke through clenched teeth. "Don't cry, or you'll look even worse." She would buy a new pair on her way to Henry Barker Productions.

She took off her tights altogether and threw them away. Then she bunched her hair into a thick ponytail and decided to leave her water-rimmed jacket in the car during her interview.

The sandwich in the café tasted like warmed-up dust, and the coffee was lukewarm water. When she had finished, Maren pushed her plate away and clutched her phone like a lifeline. She would call someone and whine a bit. It would make her feel better. She would call . . . Ton—No, no, no. She couldn't call Tony. Why on earth did his name pop up? What a confused state her brain was in.

She shook her head to get rid of the soft feeling that had surged up inside her and dialed Annie's number. Annie wasn't in. Fine. Did she have any other friends she could call in the middle of the day to indulge in a fit of self-pity?

No.

Not one.

Maren gulped. Her work and Sherry left so little time, she'd let them all slip away, too far away to call for a quick whining session out of the blue.

Her mother? Their telephone conversation had been too fraught with nerves this morning. Usually, she got along better with her mother. Besides, she needed to know how long they would stay in Spokane. She dialed the number. The phone had barely rung before her mother answered. Maren closed her eyes in relief. "Hi, Mom, it's me."

"Maren!" Her mother sounded delighted.

Maren felt the ends of her mouth pick up.

"It must be telepathy!" her mother said. "I've just thought of you."

"Really? How nice."

"Well, I wanted to talk to you about Sherry. I forgot this morning, what with one thing or another, so I made a mental note to mention it first thing we talk again."

Maren's heart sank. "Oh."

"Yes. Do you know that last Tuesday, when I picked her up after school, she wasn't wearing any underwear?"

Maren blinked. "What?"

"Yes! I saw it by chance when she put on her swimsuit and asked her about it. She said she forgot."

"She . . . she forgot?"

"Yes. And I really think you should pay a bit more attention to your child. I know you like her to be independent, but she's only a little girl, after all. You can't let her dress all by herself!"

"Mom, she has dressed herself for the past three years, and I think that's great."

"Yes, but you can't let her go to school without any underwear beneath her trousers."

"No." Maren sighed. "I assure you, I didn't do it on purpose. Did you ask her why she did it?"

"She said it looked better because the seams didn't show through."

"Oh."

"You really have to check on her, Maren."

"How? You want me to body-check her every morning?" Maren looked up.

The waiter stared at her with a curious expression.

Great. Maren averted her face.

Her mother's tone got irritated. "I want you to stay with her when she dresses! Besides, do you ever notice what she wears? Thick sweaters in summer, flimsy dresses in winter. Recently, she wore a mismatching pair of socks."

"Well, she thought that was funny."

"I see." Inga's tone could have frozen Puget Sound. She took a deep breath. "I know it's no good talking to you. You always do as you want."

The phone crackled into the silence. Maren couldn't think of anything to say.

Her mother said, "So how was the presentation?"

Maren closed her eyes. "All right. I have to go now. Bye, Mom."

She hung up, then flinched. She had forgotten to ask about Aunt Mary.

With a hollow feeling, Maren schlepped herself to the Henry Barker Productions building on East Cherry Street. On the way, she tried to buy a new pair of tights, but the drugstore at the corner of the street had been replaced by a pet food store.

Wonderful. Maren bit her lips in indecision. She had no idea where to find another drugstore. And she didn't want to be late under any circumstances. She checked her watch again. She had no choice; Henry Barker would have to live with her bare knees.

She arrived at the building with five minutes to spare. *Well, at least that's something,* Maren entered the lift. *Maybe it's my only achievement today, so I'd better be proud of it.* During the short trip to the twenty-second floor, she concentrated on ignoring her wobbly knees, which felt exposed without tights.

Maybe they wouldn't notice her strange outfit. After all, TV people were different, weren't they? Kind of freakish. Not like . . . like bankers, or . . . or tax consultants. Yes. TV people were different. She hoped.

The doors of the lift whooshed to the sides. In front of Maren, white glass walls formed an arched entrance. The logo HENRY BARKER PRODUCTIONS was etched in tiny print roughly in the area where Maren looked in vain for a door handle. Puzzled and insecure, she stepped closer.

The doors slid to the sides, whispering through the silence. Maren suppressed a nervous giggle. She felt like Alice in Wonderland.

Behind the door, another curve blocked her way. It was a reception desk made of the same glass as the door. Maren half-expected to see a mouth appear in the curve, asking her with a metallic voice about her business. But to her surprise, a human emerged behind the desk.

As soon as she saw her, Maren knew TV people were different. More glamorous. Perfect. Like Barbies come alive.

Maren advanced with grim determination, as if going into war. The receptionist pursed her pink lips as Maren handed over her business card, then gave her a sizzling smile. "Hi."

For some reason, Maren was convinced she had no idea who she was.

"Mr. Barker is still busy. You'll have to wait a few minutes."

Maren looked around. Next to the white glass walls that had closed again like a giant trap, she discovered a modern structure, about knee-high. It was made of glittering chrome profiles formed like a pretzel. Or rather, like a pretzel would look if it had an acute stomach ache. On top and roughly in the middle of the pretzel structure perched a pink plastic saucer. Maren eyed the contraption. It could be nothing but a chair.

She looked back at the receptionist, but Barbie had dived somewhere behind the glass counter. It seemed nobody was going to offer her a seat. For a moment, she remained standing, but finally, she figured she could sit down if she was left to her own devices. With care, she lowered herself onto the pretzel. At least she had no more tights to lose.

Maren waited twenty minutes. The pretzel proved to be as uncomfortable as it had looked. From time to time, a muted scratching came from behind the counter. Maybe Barbie was cleaning her nails. It was so quiet Maren wondered if the whole floor had flown to the moon, and she had somehow been taken along. At least a phone should ring or a keyboard should tap. Maybe Barbie had a trapdoor behind the counter and had disappeared onto a secret mission.

Maren suppressed another giggle and checked her watch once again. Five past three. Where on earth were they? She had a date tonight and couldn't afford to be late. Her face softened as she thought of Sherry. No doubt they were busy with last rehearsals right now. She hoped Sherry had not been too nervous to eat her lunch. A little thrill settled in her stomach. She was looking forward to seeing her daughter on stage. Then she remembered her mother's words and sighed. She tried so hard to do things right, but for some reason, she always failed. Who would ever have thought that Sherry would go to school without underwear! She would have to ask her why.

Twelve past three. Surely that was enough. She had to check if she was all alone on this planet or if the Henry Barker people had forgotten her existence.

She eased herself up, stretched her aching back, and advanced to the counter. Her heels clattered in the silence like a jackhammer.

"Em . . . hello?" She peered beneath the glass counter.

Nobody. She was all alone in the room.

Maren froze and looked for a trapdoor. Then she shook herself. Barbie must have gone out while she had been too fascinated by the pretzel. The scratching sound she had heard must have come from the fax on the desk.

She tapped her fingers on the counter. Now what?

At that moment, a white door in the background flew open and a group of people surged in like water through a broken dam. The room exploded into noise. A cell phone rang; a man with a shock of white hair shouted something at Barbie, who came running behind him; a woman with sleek black hair followed on her heels, her hands flying in all directions as she screamed at a young man with a pointed beard. "You can't do it that way! I tell you. You're dead. DEAD." Without a look in her direction, the group surged past. The glass doors slid to the side, and in another second, the wave was gone.

Maren gave a start and ran toward Barbie. "Excuse me!"

Nobody seemed to hear her. The white-haired man bellowed "Hello?" into his cell phone, and the young man shouted, "If those fools at EAP would for once do as they're told, I could make the ATP all right!"

The doors of the elevator opened.

"Excuse me!" Maren shouted and gripped Barbie's sleeve.

Barbie stared at her as if a ghost had materialized at her side.

Maren felt as if she had become invisible. "I'm supposed to have a meeting with Henry Barker at three," she shouted.

Barbie frowned, then nodded. "Yeah. But he's busy."

The black-haired woman and the young man entered the elevator.

The white-haired man shouted into the phone, "Yes! You do that!" He slipped his phone back into his jacket, then focused on Maren. His light eyes scanned her from top to toe.

Maren suppressed the impulse to hide behind the pretzel. "Ah," he said, "I know. You're The Doggy Dog Company aren't you?"

"Not quite." Maren fixed a smile on her face. "The Start-Up Company."

He frowned. "I can't recall . . . ," he said.

The doors of the lift started to close, and the woman with the black hair bent out. "You coming or not?"

"Keep your hair on." He stepped into the lift.

Barbie joined them. As the doors closed, Barbie sent

her another beaming smile and called out, "We'll be back in a sec."

Maren leaned against the wall. "I don't believe this." She walked around the pretzel five times to loosen up, then checked her watch again. Nineteen past.

"Don't panic, Maren. There's time enough." She hugged herself. The delay was still manageable. Dolly Plow had said that a meeting lasted half an hour. Even if they only started at half past, she would still have enough time and could dart out the door at four. She continued calculating her options.

If she left at five past four, it would be manageable. Just.

Seven past was the absolute limit.

Ten past meant she would have to race to the ferry.

No, whatever happened, she would have to finish the meeting at four. Darn, darn, darn. Where was the guy?

The glass doors whispered open again, and the whole group poured back into the room, still shouting at the top of their lungs. The white-haired guy waved at Maren. "You come with me! Dolly! You bring us coffee, will you?" His bellow reverberated off the wall.

Barbie nodded and disappeared through the white door.

Maren concluded he was Henry Barker. Clutching her handbag, she obeyed his summons and followed him through the white door. A strong smell of coffee assailed her.

Her guide whipped her through a white corridor and

threw open a door that led to a conference room so small, it was overcrowded with a table a bit larger than a handkerchief and three chairs. White walls, white plastic chairs, white linoleum floor, white table. The interior designer must have had a weakness for white or a rigid briefing. The only blotches of color were about six plastic coffee cups all over the table. They had left brown circles on the white laminate tabletop. Henry Barker wiped the cups to the side of the table with his sleeve and grinned.

"Have a seat," he said.

With relief, Maren obeyed. At least the chairs were comfortable.

"So." He leaned back and crossed his arms behind his head. "The Doggy Dog Company, eh? Great title." His light eyes seemed to x-ray her.

Maren narrowed her eyes. *Why does he mix me up all the time? My name is nowhere close that Doggy Dog name!* "Not quite. The Start-Up Company."

He waved his hands through the air. "Ah, yes. Now convince me why we should broadcast your profile on *Noteworthy Enterprises.* Be brief."

Maren took a deep breath and bent forward. "I founded the company because I realized that many great ideas never see the light of day due to—"

His mobile phone rang. "Excuse me." He switched it on. "Hello? . . . Yes . . . No, not at all. . . But you know her story is less interesting than my cutoff fingernails! . . . No. . . Tell her to get lost." He hung up and waved his hand at her. "Sorry. Please continue."

"Yes. As I said, many people are afraid to fight for their dreams and fear—"

The door flew open and Dolly plunked two plastic cups with steaming coffee onto the table. "Henry, you gotta come. Sandra's throwing a fit."

"Darn that woman!" He jumped up, grabbed his cup of coffee, and strode through the door. From outside, she heard a faint, "I'll be back in a sec."

Maren closed her eyes and slumped in her chair. Fourteen minutes. She still had fourteen minutes to make a pitch, to bring her company on television, to make it a success, to make a living. Fourteen minutes.

Five and a half minutes later, Maren couldn't stand it anymore. She opened the door and looked into the corridor. Henry Barker stood at one end together with the black-haired woman. For once, they whispered. It was so out of character from what she had seen so far, it sent a chill down her spine. She managed to catch his eye and smiled, hoping she didn't look like an icicle trying to be friendly.

He waved and bounced toward her. "I'd almost forgotten you, but here I am." He beamed as if he deserved a treat for being so good.

In the conference room, he dropped into his chair, jumped up again, opened the door, and shouted, "Dolly! Two more coffees, please!"

Maren clenched her fists under the table. "The Start-Up Company helps people to set up their own companies," she started with dogged desperation. "I advise on how to set up a business plan, check on the competition, consult on—"

The telephone rang again.

Maren slanted a look at her watch. It was two to four.

Henry Barker waved at her, "Continue, continue!" and answered the phone.

". . . legal issues and tax questions . . ." Her voice petered out.

"No!" he boomed into the phone, "I don't want her! How often do I have to say that? She has as much charm as a baboon! Tell her to get lost!" He hung up. "So sorry," he said. "Do go on. You were saying . . . ?"

Maren opened her mouth, but before she could utter a word, the door opened again and Dolly brought the coffee. "EAP is waiting for your call," she said. "They say it's urgent."

Henry Barker got out his phone. "You'll excuse me," he said, his eye already on the display.

Maren got up. Her stomach felt like a cold stone. "I'm sorry; I have to leave now."

His mouth dropped open. "What?"

"I particularly asked to get an appointment at three o'clock because I have another engagement that I can't cancel. I'm sorry, but I have to leave."

He shrugged. "Suit yourself. But I tell you, with that attitude, you won't get anywhere in life."

Maren narrowed her eyes and opened her mouth to wipe him from the face of the earth with a scathing answer, but at the last instant, she managed to kick down her pride. "Maybe we can arrange another date?"

He laughed. "I'm a busy man, as no doubt you realize. Some chances in life just come once." He punched in a number on his phone. She was dismissed.

Chapter Fourteen

Maren held her head high and clenched her teeth so hard, she wondered if she could ever unlock her jaw again. As if in a trance, she took the elevator down, found her car, got into it, and started the motor.

"Forget it." Her voice sounded like a foreign thing. "Forget it."

She had gone two blocks before she heard the strange bumping sound coming from the right. At the same moment, a black Chrysler next to her blared its horn. The driver gesticulated toward her front tire.

Maren stopped her car on the curb and got out. Mute, she stared at the wobbly black mass that used to be her tire.

A flat.

Tears welled up in her eyes. She tried to swallow, but her throat hurt too much. Even if she could change the wheel by herself, she would miss the ferry. She had to make it to the ferry. She had to get to Sherry's dance, come what may. Come hell or high water.

That's what she had promised.

That's what she would do.

She grabbed her handbag, locked her car, and looked around. She was in a strict no-parking zone. Her car would be towed. But it didn't matter. Nothing mattered but her promise. Nothing.

She scanned the street for a taxi. There! She waved at it, but the driver ignored her and drove on. Maren ran to the next street corner. It was ten past four. She bit her lips until she tasted blood and hailed every taxi she could see, but they all sailed past. Darn, darn, darn. A quarter past four. She might just as well give up now.

Tony dropped into the chair in his office and let out a deep breath. His legs hurt. The red light on his answering machine blinked. He bent forward. Could it be Maren? How he hoped she would call him. He had to make her talk to him. He hit the button.

"Anthony, this is your father speaking. Call me back immediately."

Tony closed his eyes for an instant. His father had spoken in a whisper. What on earth had gone wrong? He deleted the message and dialed his father's number.

"Anthony. Thank you for calling back."

Tony cringed. His father sounded as if he was smoldering. "Hi, Dad. What's the matter?"

"Don't pretend you have no idea. It would be the first time you're not in it together."

Tony swallowed. "What do you mean? Is it . . . is it something to do with Chris?"

"Indeed. It has something to do with Chris." No, his father wasn't smoldering. He was white-hot angry.

"Yes?"

"He has just handed in his notice."

Tony jumped up. His chair crashed to the ground. "What?"

"Nice performance." His father's voice dropped even lower. "But you don't need to pretend. Chris said you put him up to it."

"I did what?" Tony heard his shout echo through the office.

"You've not developed a sudden deafness, have you, Anthony?"

"But what will he do?" Tony stood rigid and stared at the wall without seeing it.

"He said he would work for the company owned by Kitty's father."

"But . . . but that's somewhere in L.A., isn't it?"

"It is. If my information is right, her father is in the movie business."

"The movie business?" Tony bent down and lifted

his chair, then dropped into it. "And what does he want to do there?"

"Chris was rather vague on that point." His father's voice sounded dry. "But he's positive about one thing, and he didn't hesitate to tell me so. His future company car will be a Mercedes convertible."

Maren hopped up and down and waved like a maniac at the next taxi.

Did it slow down?

Did it?

She held her breath.

Yes, it did!

Finally.

Before it had come to a stop at the curb, Maren threw herself headlong inside. A cloud of stale garlic air threatened to suffocate her, and her bare legs stuck to the sticky bolster. Never mind. It was a taxi, a thing from heaven. "To the Bainbridge ferry, please," she said, her breath coming in gasps. "As quick as you can."

The taxi driver threw her a look out of eyes so black, they looked liquid. Without a word, he nodded and accelerated with screeching tires. Maren sat on the edge of the seat, her hands curled into fists. They swerved to the left, then between a heavy pickup and bus. Maren jerked back. Did he know what he was doing?

Another swerve threw her against the door. If he killed her, she wouldn't be in time for the dance, either.

Thank God he slowed down. A red traffic light. The motor throbbed, frustrated, impotent. Was the light never going to change to green? There! Off they raced.

A blue flash cut into their way from the right. The driver swore and jerked at the wheel. Tires screeched. Maren clung to the bolster and pressed her eyes shut. She couldn't afford an accident; she couldn't afford any delay. No. No. No!

The motor roared in protest, then the taxi shot forward again. Maren opened her eyes. They were in the middle of the road. Which road? She had no idea. Buildings streamed by, lighted shop displays flashed. On the sidewalk, people, only a blur. Maren's fingernails burned her flesh inside her clenched hands.

Another red light. The car skidded to a stop.

I have to make it.

I have to make it.

I have to make it.

Maren tried to take a deep breath, but something heavy sat on her chest.

Green.

Off they went. On two tires, they shot into Yesler Way. Maren hung at the window. There! She could discern the white stern of the ferry, still at the pier. Yes!

With screaming brakes, the car rocketed to a halt.

Maren thrust her fifty dollar bill at the driver, one foot already out the door. "Thank you, that was brilliant!"

He threw a look at the bill, chewed his gum, and shook his head. "I don't take large bills."

She blinked. "What?"

"No big bills. You got change?"

"I . . . no. Don't you have anything? Nothing at all? A ten dollar bill, twenty dollars?" She stared at the display. The charge was $7.40. "Please?"

The driver shook his head, his face impassive. "Nah."

Maren gritted her teeth and thrust the fifty dollar bill into his hand. "Okay. Take it."

She jumped out of the taxi and raced toward the ferry, cursing the driver, cursing herself, cursing her car, cursing Henry Barker. Pain exploded in her ankle. Maren bit her lips and hobbled forward as fast as she could.

She arrived the second the ferry cast off.

Rooted to the ground, seeing it but not comprehending, she stared at the widening gap between the boat and the pier. Gray water gurgled. A plastic bottle danced on the waves, mocking her. Something cold gripped her heart and didn't let go.

Too late.

She was too late.

She broke her promise.

She'd let Sherry down.

Sherry would wait in vain for her at the dance. She would see all her classmates arrive with their parents. She would hover at the door and rake the school ground with an anxious gaze. But her mother would never come.

Tears rose hot and stinging in Maren's eyes.

No! Maren balled her fists. She couldn't let it happen.

She had to find a way. She had to, even if it meant moving heaven and earth. She could get back into her taxi and ask him to drive her to Bainbridge Island for the fifty bucks she'd already given him. Maren swiveled on her heels, ignored the pain, and raked the street with her gaze.

A green plastic bag blew across the black asphalt, otherwise . . . nothing. No trace was left of the taxi, as if she had dreamed it up.

Maren shook her head. *Never mind. Never mind.* It would have been too slow anyway. What else?

A helicopter. She needed a helicopter. Or better yet, a boat. Someone to drive her over the sound right now, right here. Maren looked up and down the pier, checking if she could find a boat, any boat, with a captain who might be persuaded to convert into a taxi driver for one trip.

The gray water snickered, as if making fun of her. One small sailing vessel, farther out. Otherwise, no one.

Maren chew the knuckles of her fist, wishing she had a white gummy bear to soothe her nerves.

Think, Maren, think! Who had a boat? Who could she call? Who could help?

She stiffened. Tony. Tony had a boat.

No way. She couldn't call Tony. Absolutely not.

"Your daughter should count more than your pride," a voice inside her said.

Maren clenched her teeth, whipped out her phone and dialed Tony's cell phone number.

"Hi, this is Tony."

"Maren here." To her horror, her voice broke and tears welled up in her eyes.

"Maren! What happened? Are you all right?"

Trust him to hear the note of desperation immediately. "I . . . tonight . . . Sherry . . . ," Maren gulped and tried to suppress a sob.

"Steady. Are you hurt?"

"I . . . no." Maren took a shuddering breath.

"Is Sherry hurt?"

"No, no, but . . . ." A sob broke out of her.

"That's fine, then." The relief in his voice was tangible. "We can handle everything else. Take a deep breath. Now, tell me."

"I missed the ferry."

"You're still in Seattle?"

"Yes. I missed the ferry." Maren banged her fist against her hip. "And Sherry's dance is tonight! I promised I would be there. I promised." Tears ran down her cheeks, impossible to check.

For a moment, he didn't say anything.

"Can you . . . could you come and pick me up in your boat?" Maren pressed the phone to her ear so hard it hurt.

He didn't answer.

Maren hurried on, "I know it's an awful lot to ask, and you don't have time, what with the restaurant and everything, but . . ."

"I would come and collect you, but I can't," he said.

"You . . . you can't?"

"No. I lent my boat to a friend. She's somewhere close to Victoria right now."

Maren slumped. "Oh, no." Sherry's face rose before her. Her little face, her anxious eyes, asking if she would come to the dance. "I can't disappoint her. I can't. I have to find a way." Her voice rose on a note of hysteria.

"When does the dance start?"

"At six."

"And it's what? A quarter to five right now?"

"Yes." Maren dropped onto the dirty curb because her legs couldn't support her anymore. "The next ferry comes at five thirty. It takes thirty-five minutes to cross the sound and another fifteen minutes to get my car and drive to the school." She felt like repeating a mantra, she'd gone through the times so often. "I'll be at least twenty minutes late. It may all be over by then. I can't do this to her." Her voice wobbled. "I promised, Tony. It's so important to her."

"Yes." He sighed. "I know. But at least your parents will be there, won't they?"

"No." Maren wiped away her tears with her left hand, a futile gesture as new ones came immediately. "They called this morning. My mother's Aunt Mary fell down the steps in her house and had to be taken to a hospital. She asked them to come and see her, and she lives in Spokane."

"Oh, no. What rotten luck. Does Sherry know?"

"Yes. She cried so hard." Maren gulped. "Do you know anybody who has a helicopter?"

"Afraid not."

"You know what's the worst?" Maren was unable to stop herself, she had to pour out her heart. "I keep seeing her face. She'll stand at the door of the auditorium, she'll check the parking lot again and again, and nobody will come. Her father never shows up anyway. She'll have nobody. All her friends will be with their families, and she'll be on her own." She pressed her eyes shut to stop the tears, but it didn't work.

"Do you . . . do you think it would help if I went?"

Maren gasped. "You?"

"Well, I know I can't replace you, but at least she won't be all on her own."

"I . . ." Maren's voice failed. "She would love it. She wanted to invite you." She caught herself midsentence. If only she hadn't said that. He would wonder why he'd never received an invitation.

"Really?" Tony sounded pleased.

"Yes. But I thought . . . Don't you have to work at the restaurant?"

"It's an emergency. I'll ask Guiseppe to stand in for me. He'll understand."

She couldn't accept it. Oh, yes, she could. Nothing mattered but Sherry. "Are you sure?"

"Yep."

"I . . ." Maren gulped again. "It would be great." She took a deep breath. "Thank you."

"Can you tell me how to find her school?" he asked.

"It's on Madison Avenue." She explained the way

with a curious mixture of relief and sadness. Long after she had hung up, she sat at the curb and stared at the water without moving. She had all the time in the world now.

Maren slid the door to the gym open by a few inches and sidled into the dark room. It smelled of rubber gym mats, as it always did, and fresh wood. The room was packed full with people, and a few dark shapes turned toward her. "Excuse me." Her whisper was inaudible because of the jazzy music. She held her breath and slipped along the wall closer to the front, where a stage had been set up. That accounted for the smell of wood. She couldn't find Tony in the darkness; she had to assume he was there, somewhere.

The stage was bright with spotlights. A little boy decorated like a tree stood in the middle, his arms spread out. Next to him crouched another boy, with slim white wooden boards fixed vertically to his side. They tapered at the top. A fence. The fence shuddered once, then sneezed so loud, it shook the lights mounted to his right. For an instant, the whole scene trembled. Maren smiled. It felt like the first spontaneous smile she'd had in a week or so.

Where was Sherry? Had she already finished her dance? She prayed not. Please. The tree threw a reproachful look at the fence. The music changed to a slower rhythm.

Two little heads lifted right and left of the tree. It

looked as if they were growing out of the stage. Maren narrowed her eyes and bent forward. How clever. The girls had been hidden in holes on the stage. Sherry and Carol lifted their faces to the crowd. Swaying with the music, they unfolded their arms as if they were petals opening to the sun.

A sheep wandered onto the stage, its woolly fleece slipping to the side. The sheep tugged it back with an impatient hiss and stopped in front of the flowers while the music picked up its pace. A drumroll beat through the gym. The sheep contemplated the trembling flowers with a hungry gaze.

Sherry's face, so serious and intent on her role, brought sudden tears to Maren's eyes. *I'm so proud of you, and I'm so glad to be here.* She didn't once avert her gaze. Maybe Sherry tried to find her in the audience, but probably she was blinded by the lights as much as she herself had been that morning at the Culinary school. How long ago it seemed. Had Sherry cried when she'd learned that her mother would be late? If only she could have spared her that experience. She had no clue what to say in her defense, later, when Sherry would confront her with the dreaded question. It would all sound like a cock-and-bull story. If you promise, you promise. That's what she had taught Sherry, and now it was coming back to haunt her.

On stage, drama was taking its course. What a challenge to find a play for twenty little boys and girls with roles neither too difficult nor too easy, neither too long nor too short. The teacher had done a great job. It ended with the dance Sherry had talked so much about. Nature made a pact, and the sheep agreed not to eat the flowers, so they all danced together. When the music stopped and the lights went out, Maren clapped her hands so hard they hurt. The lights came on again, and the kids bowed, all holdings hands. Starry-eyed and flushed, they looked as bowled over by their success as their proud parents. The applause continued. Maren stepped forward and shouted "Anchor! Anchor!"

Sherry's head whipped around. A huge smile split up her face when she discovered Maren in the dim light, then she broke out of the line, hopped from the stage, and ran straight into her mother's arms.

Maren caught her, blinded by tears. "You were wonderful!" she said into her hair. "I'm so proud of you!"

"Mommy, you shouted *anchor*!"

"But of course I did. I want to see more."

Sherry giggled.

Maren closed her eyes. Happiness flooded her. What a difference a little giggle could make.

"Mommy, you know what happened tonight?"

"No, tell me."

"Tony came! He said it was a surprise for me, and you had especially invited him, and you know what?" Her voice trembled in awe. "He brought me flowers."

Maren stared at her flushed daughter. "He brought you what?"

"A huge bunch of flowers! All pink!" Sherry slid

down and made a gesture with her arms, showing a bouquet twice her size. "This large!"

Bless him. Bless him. If he had been next to her, she would have kissed him.

"Wow!"

"Yes! And he said that's normal . . ." She giggled again, and Maren couldn't help herself, she had to join in, ". . . when you come to see a famous actress."

"He's right, of course."

"My flowers had to wait in his car, because there was no room in the dressing room, you see, but he said that's no problem, he brought a bucket with water too, because he knew I wouldn't be prepared for them."

Maren had to bite back a laugh at Sherry's worldly wisdom. "Very proper, I'm sure," she said.

"And he said you would come a bit later, but it didn't matter because we had the boring speech first. It took ages."

Thank God for the speech. "I was late," Maren said, "but I came in time for your play. I saw it right from the beginning, when the fence sneezed."

Sherry giggled again.

Maren's heart lifted. She swept her daughter once again into her arms and hugged her tight. When she looked up, she saw Tony standing in front of her, a wry smile on his lips.

"Thank you. Thank you so much." Maren tried a smile, but she knew it was too wobbly to pass. She'd never before realized how inadequate words could be.

Sherry whipped around and lunged herself into Tony's arms. "Tony!"

There. What a much better way of expressing yourself. Maren wished she could join her.

Chapter Fifteen

An hour later, Sherry had fallen asleep in the corner of the sofa while Maren described every single disaster of her day. She had kicked off her shoes and pulled up her legs onto the sofa, one arm around Sherry. Tony lay in her comfortable easy chair, his long legs stretched out before him, his gaze never leaving her face. Dusk had turned the sky to lavender blue, and through the open window, Maren heard a blackbird chirp its night song. The massive flower bouquet on the low table next to the sofa smelled sweet and summery.

". . . and then the taxi driver took my fifty bucks as if it was his due. I bet I made his day." Maren sighed. "And in spite of it all, I missed the ferry by inches."

"What a nightmare," Tony said, "but that reminds me." He put his hand into his pocket, drew out three bills and held them toward her. "There you are. It's your share of the speech."

Maren stared at the bills. "Three hundred dollars?"

Tony grinned. "Yep. It's good to be famous, isn't it?"

"But . . . but it's your money. Mr. Brown asked you, not me."

"Nonsense. We held the speech together so here's your share." When she didn't take the bills, he threw them onto the low table in front of the sofa. "But I have even better news."

Maren laughed, a laugh of sheer relief. "What can be better?"

"Mr. Brown wants us to lead a special course for the sophomores next year. With more details and hands-on practice on what we presented. He would like to combine it with internships for all the students at my restaurant. We would give two lessons per month, and each student would work five days at the restaurant."

Maren stared at him. "Did he . . . did he mention me? I mean, are you sure he offered it to both of us?"

Tony laughed. "Of course. He wants you to go into more details concerning government grants, tax relief, eating and food trends in society, and so on. He said it was a brilliant idea to combine both sides."

Happiness flooded Maren and made her so light, she thought she could float out the window. "Wow." It meant a steady income. Their speech had given her a small but firm base to build on. Her stomach filled with butterflies.

"When on earth did he tell you? After our speech, he disappeared so quickly I thought he hated it."

"He called me this afternoon."

Maren laughed again; it just bubbled out of her. "Oh." She sighed with happiness. "If you had asked me a few hours ago, I would have sworn this day was the worst in my life."

He smiled. "Do you know that your laugh is irresistible? When I got to know you, I immediately wanted to see you laugh."

Maren could feel hot blood rising to her face. "Well, you did, didn't you?"

"Not that evening. The first time was at your father's house, when I did the catering for his birthday."

"Really? What did we laugh about?"

He smiled. "I can't recall. But I had to grab the table to steady myself."

Something hot seared through Maren. She looked down and smoothed a curl of Sherry's hair from her forehead. All at once, she had to think of the woman in the car next to him. Darn.

"I wished you would laugh more often," Tony said.

She smiled. "If you continue to bring me news like this, I promise to laugh all the time."

"I have more news, but I'm not sure if it will make you laugh." He lifted both hands. "No, no, don't look like that. It's not bad news, either. Chris handed in his notice today."

"What?" Maren's mouth dropped open.

Tony grinned. "My words exactly. Remember Kitty? She's the one whose computer crashed the night I met you." His smile made her heart beat faster. "Her father is in the movie industry in Los Angeles. Chris will join his company. He'll have a Mercedes as his company car, so he's as happy as can be."

Maren rubbed her nose. "You know, I believe Los Angeles might be right for him."

"You do?"

Maren nodded. "If he works his charm, and I believe he will, he can be extremely successful."

"I hope so," Tony said. "He suffered at Mountforth and Adams, though he doesn't admit it."

"Yes. I know. How . . . how do you feel about it?"

One corner of his mouth lifted in that crooked smile she found so irresistible. "I'll miss him, in spite of it all. But he was so unhappy, and never admitted it. Any change will be better."

Maren nodded. "I agree."

Sherry mumbled in her sleep, and Maren caressed her smooth cheek.

He said, "You have a stubborn strand of hair that always falls forward and throws a shadow onto your cheek. Did you know that? It's enchanting."

"Hmm." Maren swallowed. Why did she always have to think of that woman in the car? She had to ask him. She had to. "Tony, can I ask you a personal question?"

"Sure."

"Who was the woman in the car with you?"

He sat up straight. "Who?" He frowned and shook his head. "When?"

Maren swallowed. How stupid she felt. He would think she was a jealous old hag. "On . . . on the Sunday after . . . after our first dinner."

He frowned. "On the Sunday . . . ?" Suddenly, he laughed. "Oh, now I know. Yes, I saw you too and felt awful. That was Rosalie."

"Rosalie." Maren's mouth felt parched. It sounded so exotic.

"She's Guiseppe's wife."

"Oh."

Tony drew his hand through his hair. "It was the day they had operated on Guiseppe. Rosalie doesn't drive, that's why I had to bring her home later that night."

A weight fell from her heart. "I see." Maren stared at her hands.

Tony said, "I was so sorry and hated to stand you up at that breakfast. But I couldn't call and say an emergency had come up. You wouldn't have believed me, would you?"

Maren swallowed and shook her head. "No . . . no, I'm afraid not."

"No wonder. Anyway, that's why I called Chris to take my place. He was furious with me."

"And then I was furious with him. It was a mess."

"Yes."

She stared out the window. A first star had appeared

and twinkled through the summer night. For a time, neither said anything.

Tony's gaze searched her face. "Can I ask you a personal question too?"

Maren's heart started to beat faster. "Of course."

"Why is Sherry's father never around?"

"Brad?" Maren took a deep breath. "He works for one of these big consulting companies. You know, the kind where they expect you to work eighty hours a week and see your family twice a year. In exchange, you get a fabulous salary. His supposed home is in Texas right now."

She met Tony's eyes and could see questions in them, questions he didn't voice. And because he had the delicacy not to ask, she wanted to tell him.

She sat up straighter and pushed her hair out of her face. "I met Brad in high school. He bowled me over. Even at that age, he had so much . . . personality, so much charisma. We started dating, and after high school, we both enrolled for business studies at Washington University. He was ambitious, wanted to make big money. I . . . I was ambitious too, but I wasn't ready to sell my soul in the process." Maren looked down at Sherry and touched her soft hair. "During our last year at university, his mother, who liked me a lot, was diagnosed with cancer." Maren swallowed. "It was in the terminal stage, and . . . and we knew she only had a few more months. She wanted us to get married before she died . . . so we did."

Maren caressed Sherry's hair, lost in thought. Through the open window came a soft breeze and the smell of moist earth. "When I got pregnant four months later, Brad felt trapped. He didn't want kids. He said I had become pregnant on purpose, behind his back so to speak." She looked up. "Ever heard of a girl planning a pregnancy two months before her final exams?" She shrugged. "He didn't believe me. I was sick and bone-tired all the time and just managed to scrape through and finish my degree. He was first in our class."

Maren bit her lips. She was grateful Tony didn't comment. "Our marriage didn't last much longer. He left us and filed for divorce. I moved back to my parents'. During the first years, I worked all kinds of secretarial jobs to make some money. I worked for tiny companies, for global companies. I worked for crazy nuts and well-organized maniacs. I worked in the food industry, computer industry, paper industry."

She looked up. The blue night-light had crept into the room, and he sat in shadow, but she knew he was listening. "I was lucky. It would have been much harder without my parents and my parents' money. And Sherry was happy. That was the main thing. But last year, I decided I didn't want to continue in that vein. I had seen so many disillusioned people who only went to work to count the minutes until they could go home. So I thought about it a bit, and finally, I took an extra course, asked my parents for yet more money, and set up my business."

She sighed. "I may seem a bit uptight sometimes, a bit too focused, but you understand, don't you, that I can't afford to fail?"

"I know the feeling," Tony's voice was warm. "Whenever a customer returned his plate with food untouched, I was devastated. I remember Guiseppe used to disappear for a few minutes whenever that happened, so he wouldn't have to bear me."

Maren smiled. "Is it different now?"

He answered her smile. "A bit. The fear is still there, but I know there are other reasons why people don't manage to eat." He laughed, a soft laugh that caressed her knotted-up inside like a soothing hand. "Take today, for instance. Would you have been able to eat anything if your interview with Henry Barker had taken place at Tony's?"

Maren shuddered.

"That reminds me," he suddenly said. "Shall I drive you to Seattle tomorrow morning, to salvage your car?"

"Would you do that?" Maren's heart gave a little jump. She would see him again. Tomorrow. Then she took a deep breath. "If it hadn't been for you . . ." She glanced at Sherry and touched her tousled hair. "I wanted to say thank you at the gym already, but it sounded too weak. The flowers made her all but forget me. It was such a great idea."

"You did say thank you, and it was perfectly all right."

Maren stared at him, at the line of his jaw, his dark hair falling forward. Her heart beat faster. "You took my place," she said.

He smiled. "Hmm. I seem to be predestined for this kind of thing."

He pulled up his legs, got up, and stretched. "It's late, and you've had an exhausting day. I'll see you tomorrow." He smiled at Sherry, tenderness softening his face. "You've done a great job with that kid, you know."

Maren eased herself up so she didn't wake Sherry and limped behind him to her front door in the kitchen. Her bare feet padded on the wooden boards. "My mother doesn't think so," she said. "Remember the story with the underwear?"

He laughed and turned to her. "Oh, who cares for tiny hitches like that? They're not the things that count."

Maren had to smile. She put a hand onto his arm. "Tony, I . . ." Her voice failed her.

"Yes?"

Maren cleared her throat. "I wanted to say I'm sorry for having been angry at you, because . . . because you took Chris' place at . . . at our first evening. You see, I felt so humiliated."

He looked at her hand. "I know." His voice sounded soft. "I'd have felt the same in your place."

"It was particularly bad because . . . because I liked you so much, right from the beginning." She didn't manage to admit she had fallen for him before she even knew what was happening.

"So did I."

"You . . . you did?" She dared to lift her gaze to his, and the expression in his eyes made her heart race.

"Yes. And ever since I've been trying to untangle the mess, but I never seemed to get anywhere."

"I think . . ." Maren's voice was a whisper. ". . . I think it's untangled now."

His dark face swam before her for an instant, then she felt his lips on hers, warm and firm. Something hot and light ran through Maren, lifted her off her feet, shook the floor beneath her.

A soft plopping sound made them jump.

Tony's hand shot up to his head, and with a suppressed oath, he untangled something out of his hair. "What on earth . . . ?"

Maren stared at the bright red paste in his hands, then broke into a peal of laughter. "Oh, no. It's Sherry's modeling clay! She threw it up to the ceiling a few weeks ago, and it got stuck." She frowned and tried to remember. "You know what? It was the day I got to know you."

Tony grinned. "But how fitting to come down right now!" He drew Maren close again. "Sometimes things take a bit longer to become unstuck."